Wendell, Santa's Lost Elf

D1468501

Wendell, Santa's Lost Elf

A Novel

Michael J. Bosco
*Author of **Roodee, The River's End***

iUniverse, Inc.
New York Lincoln Shanghai

Wendell, Santa's Lost Elf
A Novel

iUniverse books may be ordered through booksellers or by contacting:

iUniverse
2021 Pine Lake Road, Suite 100
Lincoln, NE 68512
www.iuniverse.com
1-800-Authors (1-800-288-4677)

Because of the dynamic nature of the Internet, any Web addresses or links contained in this book may have changed since publication and may no longer be valid.

This is a work of fiction. All of the characters, names, incidents, organizations, and dialogue in this novel are either the products of the author's imagination or are used fictitiously.

ISBN: 978-0-595-45090-9 (pbk)
ISBN: 978-0-595-69179-1 (cloth)
ISBN: 978-0-595-89401-7 (ebk)

Printed in the United States of America

To my parents: Marylou and Joe Bosco. When I was ten years old we moved out into the country with all the horses, cows, pastures, ponds, streams, the plateau, and the roaming hills. This was my inspiration to become a writer, and for that, I thank them.

Love,
Mike

A special thanks to: My wife Sue for all she puts up with, her inspiration, her dedication, and her desire to edit everything I write. Also, a big thanks to Chris Johnson for reading my manuscript and pointing out my flaws.

Prologue

O n Christmas Eve 1896, Wendell was ready to embark on the ride of a lifetime, something he'd dreamed about for as long as he could remember. This adventurous night was to be for him *alone*, without anyone else sharing or stealing his glory, and he won the experience fair and square. Out of all the elves up at the North Pole, he was the lucky one. His time had finally come. He'd won the lottery, and as the other elves were busily loading the last few presents onto the sleigh, Santa looked over at Wendell, patted him on the shoulder, and gave him a wink.

Wendell wasn't what you would call your typical "jolly old elf," or an overly happy elf, or even a well-known elf. He was more of a quiet, busy-at-work, stay-out-of-trouble, shy type of elf with just a handful of close friends. Every year, at least for the last one hundred or two, a lottery was held to pick that one lucky elf to assist Santa Claus during his Christmas Eve ride around the world. Santa decided long ago that taking someone along to help with the bazillion deliveries would make his job much easier.

Once the sleigh was ready, Santa grabbed hold of the reins, gave another quick wink and a wave to all the elves, and yelled out "Merry Christmas!" When the reindeer heard those words, they immediately took to the skies, and then they were out of sight in two blinks.

As Wendell looked about, everything seemed a blur. The reindeer were running at a normal pace, and Santa's voice, as he called out to them, was normal, But everything around them was moving at an astonishing speed.

"Don't worry Wendell," Santa assured him. "It's completely safe … just takes a little getting used to. You're doing fine."

"Thank you, Santa. By the way, how will I be assisting you tonight?"

"It's simple, Wendell. Every time I stop the sleigh, you'll reach into the bag and pull out the first present you touch."

"How will I know if I grabbed the right gift?"

"You will; that's the beauty of this process, Wendell. It's magic."

During the first five minutes, Wendell couldn't believe that he handed Santa over ten thousand presents, and he wasn't even tired! The night was, indeed, full of magical surprises. Everything was running like clockwork … absolutely perfectly.

After what seemed like several hours, Wendell started to get bored with the same old routine of waiting for the sleigh to stop before he grabbed the next present, and he decided to start collecting them while the sleigh was still in flight. While this seemed to work well for the second half of the night, and Santa didn't seem to have a problem with the change in procedure, something was about to happen that would forever alter Wendell's life.

With only a few thousand more presents to deliver, Wendell hopped up onto the seat, and instead of reaching for the next present, he decided to pull out his pocket watch to check the time. This turned out to be a huge mistake. When he reached into his pocket to pull out his watch, he did so with his left hand, the hand he'd been using to hold himself steady on the seat. At that very moment, Santa pulled the left rein toward him to bank the sleigh left as he descended over a mountain, within that split second, without Santa knowing what happened, Wendell was tossed out of his seat and over the edge.

When Santa brought the sleigh to a stop, he reached back to Wendell to get the next package, but Wendell wasn't there. Santa immediately jumped up onto the seat and searched in every corner of the sleigh.

"Wendell!" Santa yelled. But there was no answer. Santa jumped out of the sleigh and made a quick search of the area, but still, there was no sign of Wendell.

For the remainder of Christmas Eve, Santa had no choice but to continue on his way, until the very last present was delivered. Then he quickly flew back to the last spot where he last remembered speaking to Wendell. There he circled the area over and over again. As long as Wendell's pocket watch was still chained to Wendell, there was hope of finding him. An elf's specially designed pocket watch and chain are intended to serve as a lifeline; it's the one thing that keeps an elf forever young. The watches have magical devices built in that give off a signal in case an elf gets lost, as long as the watch remains intact and attached to the elf. But if the watch and chain become separated, there's no longer a signal. After several passes and no signal or sign of Wendell, Santa feared that his favored elf and the elf's watch had become separated. If this turned out to be true, Santa knew that Wendell would be lost forever. Feeling very sad at the end of this magical night, he slowly guided his reindeer through the sky and back to the North Pole.

Chapter One

A warm summer breeze drifted through the window as Josh sat
at his desk, counting down the minutes while his sixth grade
teacher, Mrs. Ford, lectured the students about what they should
and shouldn't do during summer vacation. Josh glanced over his
shoulder at his best friend Billy and held up three fingers to signal
how many minutes were left before the semester's final bell would
ring.

The year was 1952. The location was a small logging town called
Whispering Pines. It's situated on the north side of the Adirondack
Mountains, in upstate New York, about forty-five miles south of the
Canadian border. This town was once the thriving home to count-
less lumber mills and the makers of some of the finest furniture in the
northeast.

More than thirty-five percent of the population of Whispering
Pines is still employed by one of those two industries today.

With a population of over five thousand, nearly every male in
town over the age of seventeen either works as a lumberjack, labors
in the lumber mills, or crafts furniture. The work is hard, and the hours
are long, but you couldn't find higher paying jobs within a hundred
mile radius.

Every kid in the classroom was getting fidgety. The school year
was nearly over, just one more minute to go. Josh repeatedly looked

across the room, waiting for Billy to leap up out of his seat to make that last dash for the door. The two boys always raced to see who could get through the door first. Billy was a couple of inches taller than Josh and outweighed him by more than twenty pounds, so he usually won the race through the doorway. But if the hallway was clear, Josh could easily run Billy down and pass him before they reached the double doors leading outside. The kids at school said that Josh ran like a jackrabbit being chased by a hound dog.

Josh, at first glance, appeared to be your typical thin, average height, redheaded, shy, twelve year old, but in fact he was much more. He was, by far, the brightest kid in school, but very few were aware of that fact. He was also a bookworm, a trait he acquired from his mom, and read just about everything he could get his hands on. His sports interest was limited though, with baseball being the only one he favored.

Billy, on the other hand, was the same age as Josh, but quite the opposite. Billy was the taller, chubby, freckled-faced, blond-haired boy whose only fear was books. He hated to read, despised studying and constantly bugged Josh for last minute help with his homework. But even though he didn't like to read, he did like thumbing through a good comic book now and then ... with a vivid imagination, a picture goes a long way.

Suddenly the bell rang. Josh and Billy jumped up out of their chairs, pushing and shoving their way to the door, but just as Josh was about to grab the doorknob, the teacher stopped everyone.

"Just one more thing before you leave, class" Mrs. Ford shouted, as she placed her hand against the door. "Don't forget to clean out your lockers before you leave the building, because if you don't, the janitor will clean them out for you and throw everything away. Have a great summer vacation, and be careful out there."

While Billy rushed to clear out everything from his locker, he yelled over at Josh to see if he wanted to take the *long* way home. The *long* way home was their "secret code" for following the trail behind the school that led up to the plateau, down the old lady's road and through downtown's main street to get home. Very few kids at school ventured up there, mostly because there were "*No Trespassing*" signs posted everywhere. Fortunately for Billy, his dad was good friends with Big John Jacobs, the farmer who owned most of the property, and he gave Billy permission to go up there anytime he wanted.

As Josh and Billy rounded the front of the school, they cut through the playground and walked along the barbed wire fence, which separated the schoolyard from the cow pasture, as they looked for the easiest place to climb over. The weeds had grown so high and thick up against the fence that the boys had difficulty finding a sturdy enough post to climb. When they finally spotted a way over, Billy went first. But when he vaulted the wire, he came within inches of landing in a huge pile of fresh cow manure. The heat of the sun pounding down escalated the smell to an almost unbearable level.

Big John Jacob's cows were herded beneath the shade of several apple trees that grew scattered about the pasture. Manure flies, as Billy calls them, were everywhere ... in the manure, on the cows, even buzzing around the boy's heads, until they finally reached the base of the plateau.

There's one particular way the boys preferred getting up to the plateau, and that was the steep narrow path that wound upward through the trees. The greatest challenge was securing a grip on the rocks and small stumps while they raced each other to the top. Josh would win ninety-nine percent of the time, as long as he could stay more than an arm's length away from him. Billy liked to grab on to Josh's belt loop any chance he could, just so he could reach the top first. This may have been cheating, but the tactic was always fun.

After making their way to the plateau's highest point, they followed the deer trail that ran along the tree line. Tall weeds surrounded the trail on either side, while just up ahead a sea of young

Indian corn blanketed several acres. It had been grown and harvested by Jimmy Smith for more than twenty years on the same plot of land that was owned by Big John Jacobs. The majority of the plateau was used for growing hay and alfalfa, in rotating years, and the few acres of land that Jimmy Smith used for his Indian corn was just an extra piece of land that Big John Jacobs never had a use for. It's rumored that this same plot of land was originally used by the Mohawk Indians, hundreds of years ago, to grow their own corn.

"Look," said Billy, as he pointed down a row of corn. "Look how tall the stalks are getting."

Within seconds, they were standing in the middle of the cornfield and inspecting the stalks, which were only about ten inches high. But Billy had to impress Josh with his vast knowledge about the planting and growing of Indian corn ... all the stuff he'd learned from Jimmy Smith.

"This is going to be real Indian corn, Josh. You know, it's that multicolored corn that people hang on their front door during the fall. These stalks will grow to over eight feet high. When all the stalks and leaves turn brown and start to die, Jimmy Smith and I will come up here and harvest all this. Then we bundle it all up, and he'll sell it down in front of his feed store."

"When will that be?" Josh questioned.

"I can't remember. I think last year it was sometime after we started back to school. He always calls the house about a week ahead of time, just to make sure I don't have any other plans. This will be my third year helping. Picking that corn is hard work, you know. Hey, you want me to ask Jimmy if *you* can help this year. He'll pay you."

"Yeah ... how much ..." Josh queried, with a gleam of excitement in his eyes.

"Last year he gave me a quarter for every bushel basket I filled, and he'll probably pay you about the same."

"Heck yeah I'll help. I sure could use the extra dough. Say, when are you going to ask him, Billy?"

"Next time I see him."

After venturing through several rows of corn stalks, the boys made their way back to the trail and headed toward the ravine. The ravine was a large area of the hill that was carved out by the melting glaciers millions of years ago and divided the plateau into two sides. The left side belonged to Big John Jacobs, while the right side was the property of the old lady that lived in a decrepit old house located at the base of the plateau. The ravine extended from the base of the plateau up through the hills for many miles. The hills towered a thousand feet above the plateau in a collage of pine, birch, and maple trees that continued for over twenty miles in either direction.

There was a small dirt road that started from the edge of town, past the old lady's house, and ended at the base of the plateau. From there, a narrow grass-covered road, barely wide enough for a small farm tractor to fit began its trek up the plateau for fifty yards before it split off into two directions. One side wound up through Big John Jacobs side while the other took a sharp right over an old logging bridge and up through the old lady's side.

At the bottom of the ravine there was a spring fed creek that began its journey several miles away at the top of the hill, traveled under the old logging bridge, continued behind the old lady's house, and ended up in Big John Jacob's seven acre pond. The water was always cold as ice, even in the middle of summer.

After the boys left the cornfield and continued along the trail, two rabbits suddenly darted out from the brush not fifteen feet in front of them, and sped off through the tall weeds, heading straight toward the ravine. Billy and Josh immediately sprang into action and took off running after them.

"Slow down," Billy said, as he stopped to catch his breath while waving his arms, motioning for Josh to move in slowly toward the ravine.

As the rabbits stopped next to a tree at the top of the ravine, Josh and Billy quietly inched their way toward them. But just as Billy got within ten feet of them, he stepped on a twig, and frightened the rabbits away. The rabbits quickly darted past the trees and disappeared down into the ravine. Just past the tree line, the boys watched as the two small animals sped toward the log bridge that spanned over the stream. Josh suddenly charged down over the steep ravine and zigzagged his way through the trees as if he had roller-skates on. Meanwhile, Billy leaned against a tree, utterly amazed at Josh's speed as he zipped across the old log bridge.

"Go, Josh go!" Billy yelled, as he began to shuffle his way toward the bottom of the ravine. When he finally reached the log bridge, Josh was clean out of sight.

Josh got a big kick out of chasing rabbits, which was also a great opportunity to get back at Billy for all those times he cheated to beat him out of the classroom. As Billy began trudging up the old logging road to get up to the plateau, he heard Josh yelling.

"Billy, get up here!" Josh shouted from afar. "Hurry"!

Suddenly, Billy started to panic. *Josh is either hurt or he caught one of the rabbits.* Billy thought to himself. Billy started running up the old logging road as fast as he could. When he reached the plateau, all he could see was an ocean of tall weeds and vine-covered trees.

"Josh ... Josh, where are you?"

"Billy, I'm over here! Come see what I've found!"

Billy followed Josh's voice through the tall weeds and overgrown bushes toward an expanse of large pine trees. Suddenly, when he emerged from the underbrush, he saw Josh standing next to a large pile of what seemed to be old barn wood.

"Wow!" Billy exclaimed. "What *is* all this?"

"I'm not sure. Looks like it used to be a cabin."

This was the first time the boys had ever ventured up to the "forbidden" side of the plateau. About two years ago when the boys were walking down the dirt road past the old lady's house, she stopped them to ask where they were going. When they told her they were going up to the plateau for the day, she quickly assured them that the plateau behind her house was her personal property and that no one was ever allowed up there. She also said that if she ever caught them up there, she would tell their parents.

"Josh, we need to hurry up and get out of here. We're not even supposed to be on this side of the plateau. Don't you remember what that old lady said? She really will tell our parents you know, she wasn't kidding. I'd be grounded for the rest of the summer if my parents knew I was up here messing around, especially when the old lady already gave you and I fair warning."

"I don't care about that, Billy. This is the neatest thing we've ever found up in these hills. I think we should stay and look around for a while. This might be the last chance we have to come up here. Let's just explore a little bit. Maybe we'll find something interesting."

The boys circled around the old dilapidated structure several times, before Billy decided to crawl up onto the roof to see if he could find a hole to peek through. The structure looked like someone walked up to the front door and pushed the whole wall in. The large, mangled wood-shake roof had collapsed inward and completely covered the back wall. The front wall and door, with a window on each side of it, were only partially covered by the roof. The right side wall was pushed outward and leaned warped and severely distorted against two trees.

The partially rotted front door and wall was half buried in the ground, but still intact, while pieces of jagged glass littered the inner sides of the window casings, resembling rows of shark teeth. Several small trees had sprouted up through the openings in the roof, while weeds and vines grew around the doorway and windows. The windows were oddly shaped, unlike your common house windows, with rounded corners instead of the typical square shape. Rocks from the chimney had apparently been hurled through the air during the collapse, and they lay scattered beyond the point where the front porch structure once stood. The poles that had supported the porch roof were half buried in the ground and lay perpendicular to the front of the structure. Each pole was covered in a collage of small carvings, which were difficult to distinguish in the soft rotting wood.

"This is great," Billy said, as he walked around lifting up loose boards to peek underneath. "I've never seen anything like this before. Who do you think might have lived here?"

"I don't have any idea, Billy, but maybe this old cabin is the reason why the old lady didn't want us coming up here."

"Yeah, I think you're right, Josh. Maybe there's something buried underneath all this. Maybe it's gold or money! This could have been somebody's hideout. That's why she didn't want us snooping around up here."

They both looked at each other with adventure in their eyes. Big smiles emerged on their faces, as if they had already discovered something valuable.

Billy continued to grab boards and crumpled up pieces of rotted wood, in hopes of finding evidence of hidden treasures. Josh started to help, but suddenly realized that it was getting late and he needed to get home for supper. Josh's mom was a stickler about having supper ready at exactly four o'clock. That's when his dad normally came home from work. She had a tendency to get upset when her routine was disrupted.

"Hey, let's come back up here tomorrow," Billy insisted. "I'll bring a crowbar and a couple of hammers to clear all this wood away so we'll be able to see what's underneath."

"What about the old lady, Billy? She'll squeal on us if she catches us sneaking back up here. This is her property, you know!"

"We'll just tell her that we're building a fort over on Big John Jacob's side of the plateau. She won't know the difference. Once we pass her house, she won't be able to see what side of the plateau we went up anyway. The trail coming up here is hidden behind all those trees in her yard. It would be impossible for her to see us crossing the log bridge from her front porch."

"What if she gets suspicious one day and waits for us on the other side of the log bridge?"

"I don't think *that's* ever going to happen. Have you ever seen her come down from that front porch before? She practically sleeps there. Besides, when she does get up, she has to use that cane to get around. So I don't think she's in that good of shape to be walking up in these hills trying to catch us crossing the bridge."

Josh finally agreed with Billy's reasoning and they started back down the hill. As they walked over the log bridge and onto the dirt road, they could see the old lady's house. Her cats were scattered all over the place, walking along the porch railing, and laying on the steps. Several were playing in the yard, and a couple were chasing each other around an old dilapidated Ford pickup truck barely visible within the tall weeds in the side yard.

The old lady spotted the boys soon after they came into view, but continued to rock in her chair as if she didn't even notice them. As soon as the boys walked directly in front of her house, she looked straight at them.

"You two youngsters stop right where you are and get on over here! I want to speak to you!" she shouted, as she scooted to the end of her rocker and leaned forward onto her cane.

Josh and Billy froze in their tracks. They didn't know what to do. How could she possibly have known they were up on her side of the plateau! Billy bravely made the first move toward her, while Josh followed close behind as they slowly shuffled their way across the flat stones leading to the front porch. As they walked up the steps, several cats quickly swarmed around their legs making it difficult to move about. While they stood near the edge of the porch with their eyes pointed down at the floor, the old lady swiftly smashed her fly swatter against a fly on the arm of her chair. The sudden strike of the swatter instantly snapped the boys to attention.

"Well ... did you find it?" the old lady asked, in an unexpectedly excited voice.

The boys gave each other a puzzled look.

"Find what, ma'am?" Josh responded, his voice soft and shaky.

"Well, Wendell's gold chain of course! Did you find it? I know you've been up there on my side of the plateau snooping around his old cabin. I could hear you two carrying on clear down here."

Josh had no clue what chain she was talking about or even who Wendell was. But he knew she expected an answer, and quick.

"No ma'am. We just got out of school today and took the long way home through Big John Jacob's side of the plateau. That's all. We don't know anything about a Mr. Wendell's gold chain. We don't even know who Mr. Wendell is, ma'am. Honest, we really don't."

The old lady sat back in her chair and stared at the boys with a blank look on her face, as though she were looking straight through them. Then suddenly, she turned her head and looked up toward the plateau. More than a minute had passed before she looked back at the boys.

"Well, you two should be running along now. It's getting late, and your parents will be worried sick. But you make sure you come by here when you find that chain of Wendell's. *Sure would like to see the look on his face when you find his gold chain,*" the old lady whispered, looking back up toward the plateau again. "Yup, sure would like to see that," she whispered again.

As the boys turned and walked down the porch steps and across the flat stones to the dirt road, they could hear the creaking of boards as the old lady resumed rocking. They were several minutes down the dirt road before either one spoke a word. The last time they were confronted by the old lady, she warned them not to cross the bridge onto her side of the plateau. But this time, she didn't yell at them at all. She was like a totally different person.

"Billy, do you know anybody named Wendell?"

"Not me. I never even heard that name before! I think she's just crazy or something. It's probably a name out of a book she read, or maybe even the name of a relative or something."

"Maybe, Billy. But just the same, do you think she really knew we were up on her side of the plateau looking around and all?"

"I don't doubt it. But even if she did, she didn't seem to care too much about it now. All she seemed to care about was that gold chain that belonged to that Wendell fellow."

"Yeah, you're probably right, Josh. She didn't even threaten us like she did last time. Maybe that's a good sign!"

"A sign of what?" Josh questioned.

"I mean maybe she doesn't remember us from before. She's like a hundred years old you know. My grandma has problems remembering stuff, too. She's probably about the same age as the old lady. Last time we went to my grandma's house, she thought I was the neighbor's boy. Mom said she just got a little confused. Anyway, I'm pretty sure we're in the clear to come back up here tomorrow."

"Yeah, Billy, but when we walk past here in the morning with our crow bars and hammers, and she stops us to ask where we're going, we're just going to tell her that we're building a fort on Big John Jacob's land. Okay?"

"Sure, Josh. Heck, she probably won't even be up at six in the morning. You know how some of those old people like to sleep late in the morning."

When the boys got to the end of the old lady's dirt road, they turned right and headed straight down Main Street to grab a couple drinks from the pop machine in front of Stub Hammond's Hardware store. While they sat on the wooden bench beneath the store window, enjoying their drinks, Josh brought up the subject of food and what they should take with them on their adventure the next day. Billy volunteered to bring the pop and a tin full of Charles Chips. Josh said he would make the peanut butter and jelly sandwiches.

After everything was decided, Josh suddenly remembered about dinner. He turned around, jumped onto the bench and pressed his face against the window. He cupped his hands next to his temples to keep the light out so that he could look through to the back wall where the big clock hung. "It's ten minutes after four!" Josh yelled. Then he spun around, jumped down off the bench, and took off running down the sidewalk.

"I have to get going, Billy," he hollered back over his shoulder. "I'm late for dinner. I'll see you tomorrow morning at six at the top of the old lady's road. Don't forget to bring the hammers and the pop."

Chapter Two

*J*osh had set his alarm for 5:30 a.m. but woke up about ten minutes ahead of time. He'd dreamed he and Billy were digging for buried pirate treasure that lay beneath the old collapsed cabin on the plateau. He woke up just as they lifted a large flat rock lying at the center of the dirt floor. Now that he was up, he couldn't wait to get up to the plateau to start digging for real.

He walked to his closet and grabbed an old pair of dungarees and the blue paint-speckled shirt he wore a few months ago when he helped his dad paint the garage. After he got dressed and brushed his teeth, he rushed down to the kitchen and ate a bowl of cereal before anyone got up. When he finished, he ran back up stairs and grabbed his lucky Brooklyn Dodgers baseball cap. It was the same hat he wore two years ago when he found a two-dollar bill on the floor as he and his mom walked into the Sears and Roebuck store, and he'd worn it ever since thinking that someday it would bring him good luck again.

After he walked back down stairs and back into the kitchen, he heard the front door close. Suddenly, his mom strolled into the kitchen after going out to the front porch to get the milk.

"Good morning Josh, what are you doing up so early? I thought you'd be sleeping late on your first day of summer vacation. Do you and Billy have something special planned for today?"

"Yeah, kind of, Billy and I decided yesterday that we'd go for a hike in the woods. I thought I'd make us some peanut butter and jelly sandwiches. You know, in case we get hungry and don't want to come all the way back home to get something to eat."

"I think that's a great idea, Josh," she replied, as she pulled down on the bill of his baseball cap on her way to the coffee pot. "Hey, take a couple of those apples from the fruit bowl on the dining room table before they go bad. You can also have some of those peanut butter cookies I baked last night. Just make sure you share them with Billy. And be careful up in those woods! I don't want you coming home all banged up like you did last year. That cost us nearly six dollars for Doctor Gray to stitch you back up. Well, I'm going upstairs to take my shower," she said, giving him a kiss on the cheek. "Oh, one more thing before I forget, I'm working late tonight, so dinner won't be ready until five. You can invite Billy over if you'd like. Just make sure he clears it with his mom first."

Josh stuffed everything from the kitchen counter into his backpack and quickly slipped out the back door. He walked as quietly as he could through the back yard so he didn't wake his dog Toby, but as soon as he passed the doghouse, Toby came charging out.

"Sorry boy, not today! I've got way too much to do, and you'll just be in the way. Maybe next time you can come with me, Toby boy."

The sun was just beginning to peek over the horizon when Josh arrived at the top of the old lady's road. He sat quietly and listened to the sound of squeaky wheels for several minutes before Billy finally appeared from around the corner. He was pulling the little red American Flyer wagon he used to play with as a youngster.

"Billy, I thought we were going to meet here at six sharp. Where have you been?"

"Sorry, Josh, I was trying to find my dad's other crow bar. I was sure he had two of them. I figured if we had two crow bars and two hammers we'd be able to tear that cabin apart in no time at all. I guess we'll just have to share this one. At least I found these two hammers."

"You look pretty silly pulling your old wagon down the road Billy. Isn't that your little sister's wagon?"

"Very funny, Josh. As a matter of fact, my mom and dad use it when they do yard work."

"Did you remember to bring the pop and chips, Billy?"

"Yup, I grabbed two bottles for each of us and a whole tin of Charles chips. I threw this old blanket over the wagon so my mom wouldn't see me take the tin. She'd get mad if she found out that I took it out of the house. That Charles chip guy charges a dollar deposit on this tin. I'll be in big trouble if anything happens to it, so make sure you remind me not to leave it up on the plateau."

"Yeah, my mom gets weird about those tins, too. She usually opens the lid for me so I don't accidentally drop it on the floor and dent it."

"Well, let's get going, Josh. We have lots of work to do. What time do you have to be home?"

"My mom said dinner wouldn't be ready until five, but said you could join us, if it's okay with your mom."

"Gee, wish I could, Josh, but we're going over to my grandparent's house for dinner."

"That's okay, Billy, maybe next time."

After they got up to the plateau and saw the old dilapidated cabin for the second time, the place actually looked bigger than the day before. They quickly realized it would take a lot longer than one day to clear the roof away; probably more like three or four. Billy grabbed the hammers out of the wagon and handed one to Josh. They immediately started tearing the wooden shingles off the roof and had quickly accumulated a good size pile. Most of the top layers had dried out over the years, but as they dug deeper, the shingles were moist and covered with green, brown, and white slimy mold. Once in a while they would spot a centipede or two, some roaches, and some unusual bugs they'd never seen before, but none of that bothered them.

Last year when Josh and Billy took a hike in the woods, Josh found an orange lizard crawling up a tree and thought he'd take the little reptile home to live in the glass bowl, as company, for his pet turtle. After several attempts, he was finally able to snatch the lizard from the tree. Then he shoved it into his coat pocket and zipped it up. Throughout that day, with all the fun he and Billy were having hiking around through the woods, he completely forgot about the lizard. Five months later when the weather started getting cold again, he pulled that same jacket out of the closet to wear to school. On the way there, he reached into the pocket and pulled out the lizard he'd forgotten about. The poor thing looked like a long dried-up raisin. He felt so bad that when he got home from school he buried the little thing in the back yard.

By ten in the morning, after almost four hours of yanking on shingles and fighting off all the weird-looking bugs in the process, Billy was finally able to reach through a hole in the roof and touch the dirt floor, which seemed to be solidly packed and dry as a bone. So even though the cabin had caved in, the roof had continued to keep everything underneath surprisingly free of water damage.

While they sat on the only visible section of exposed rock footing, munching on Charles chips and enjoying a few sips of pop, Josh noticed something bright red sticking out from under one of the boards, lodged under the front wall. The object appeared to be a piece of material. Josh jumped up, grabbed hold of it, and started pulling. But the fabric was caught on something and was too thick to even tear. After they finished their snack, they began concentrating on removing the wood lodged around the piece of red material so they could get it out.

The more they imagined about what the material could be, the faster they worked. Eventually, after moving just about everything that was lying on top, they were able to dig out all the heavily compressed dirt. Billy shook the dirt off and quickly realized that the red piece of fabric was actually a pair of pants. He held them up to his waist to see how they looked and began dancing around acting silly. The pants were *way* too big in the waist, and the legs were so short they didn't even reach down to his ankles.

"Who do you think these could have belonged to?" Billy asked, as he began frantically searching through the pockets.

"I don't know," Josh Laughed, they look like something a short chubby clown would wear. Who else would *wear* something like that?"

Billy wadded them up and tossed them aside. Then he and Josh got back to work. A few minutes later, Josh pulled up a loose board from the front wall and spotted a small, peculiar-looking wooden object lying on the dirt floor. When he reached through and pulled the object out into the light, he couldn't believe what he'd found. It was a perfectly preserved *detailed* wood carving of a squirrel. It couldn't have been any more detailed; even the eyes looked real. It was as though they were actually staring back at him. The squirrel's mouth was wide open, ready to attack the nut he held with its front paws.

The treasure hunt was going just as they figured it would. They had already found their first piece. It wasn't the chest full of pearls or bags full of gold coins they'd hoped for, but it was a good start. They sat down on a couple dried-out planks of wood and ate their lunch while they admired their big find that was perched on top of the Charles chips tin. After lunch, they continued pulling off as many boards as possible before it was time to leave for the day.

As they walked past the old lady's house on their way home, they looked up at the porch and noticed her sitting in her chair, rocking back and forth. She didn't speak or even turn her head. She just rocked back and forth.

When Sunday morning arrived, Billy and Josh went to church with their families. After church, they all went back to their houses and ate a late breakfast. This had been their normal Sunday ritual for as long as the boys could remember. This was how Sundays were supposed to be. Once Josh finished eating, he ran up to his room to change into his old clothes. Then he dashed out the back door and cut through all the neighbors' yards to Billy's house, which was the fastest way to get there.

Billy was already busy in his garage loading up the wagon when Josh came around the corner. Besides the hammers and the crowbar, he threw in a flashlight, a shovel, and some old towels to wrap up the squirrel and any other items they might happen to dig up. Then he finally located the second crowbar. As they left the garage and start heading down the driveway, Billy's little sister Suzy ran up behind Billy and grabbed his hand.

"Go back to the house, Suzy," Billy said, as he took her by the arm and walked her around to the back yard. "Suzy, I told you before, you're too young to go up in the woods with Josh and me. When you get a little bit bigger, I promise I'll take you with us. But for now, you need to stay here and play in the backyard."

"Okay," Suzy replied softly, looking up at Billy with tears in her eyes. "I stay right here till you get back, Billy."

It was close to 11 0'clock as they scurried down the dirt road past the old lady's house. This was one of those rare occasions when she wasn't on the porch rocking away in her chair. She was probably in her house taking a nap. Wasn't even noon, yet the hot and muggy day was at its peak. Luckily, when they crossed the log bridge it was ten degrees cooler in the shade. Walking up the trail toward the plateau, they could feel the heat again in the areas where the sun spiked through the trees. By the time they finally reached the plateau and moved into the clearing, beads of sweat were steadily dripping down their faces. The weatherman wasn't predicting any rain for the next few days, so the boys had at least three more days of dry digging before everything would get too soggy.

Before they started digging, Billy pointed the flashlight down through another hole he spotted in the roof. Scattered around on the dirt floor below, he saw a small table and a couple of chairs off toward the corner of the room, which appeared to have been completely flattened by the weight of the roof. Other smaller items were partially covered by debris and difficult to make out.

The boys worked steadily for the next three hours and were able to clear nearly half the roof away. More and more of the cabin floor became visible, along with the rock footing where the cabin once rested. There was a large odd-looking wooden structure, which was still partially covered by one of the walls that resembled a bed that was tucked up against the corner of the room. After they removed a few more boards, they could see the footboard and part of the frame. The footboard had a carving of a Christmas wreath with intertwining branches around two pine cones and a large bow at the top. In the center of the wreath was a distinctive carving of the letter **W**.

"*Wendell,*" Josh whispered. "This bed must have belonged to that Wendell fellow the old lady was talking about."

"Why would he leave his bed here?" Josh asked.

"Maybe he didn't leave it," Billy said, in a spooky sounding voice. "Maybe he died when the cabin collapsed in on top of him, and all that's left are his bones. They're probably still lying in the bed."

Josh immediately turned around, jumped over the rock wall, and started running.

"Josh!" Billy yelled, "I'm only kidding with you! Come back here and help me pull some more of these boards off!"

Josh slowly walked back and stood on the outside of the rock wall.

"What if he really is under there, Billy?"

"I don't know! I guess he'd be all full of worms and bugs and all rotted and stuff,"

"Billy!"

"Okay, okay. Maybe he's not under there. Maybe he just moved into a bigger house in town somewhere and bought all new furniture. Let's just keep working, Josh. It's almost time to head for home."

After another hour of pulling up boards and searching the floor for more treasures, Billy finally said, "Let's get everything loaded back into the wagon, Josh. We have to get going. Oh, by the way, I won't be able to come up here again until Wednesday or Thursday. My dad's on vacation this week, and he wants me to help him build a new fence around the backyard."

"You'll be busy for two days?" Josh complained. "That's not fair. We finally find something neat to do up here, and you get stuck with helping your dad. Well, I guess I'll just have to wait until Wednesday, because I'm not coming back up here by myself."

"Don't forget, Josh," Billy said, as they walked past the collapsed cabin, "according to the old lady, that gold chain of Wendell's was lost somewhere up around this area. Might even be buried underneath all this wood. But in any case, we're going to find it!"

Chapter Three

For the next couple of days, rain fell incessantly. The Weatherman was wrong once again. So, instead of Billy helping his dad build a new fence around the back yard, he helped him clean out the garage and the basement. By Wednesday, the rain had stopped, and Billy and his dad were in the backyard taking measurements and staking out locations for the new fence posts.

Josh, on the other hand, was starting to get bored after being cooped up in the house for two days and decided to venture on over to Billy's house to see if he could help with the fence. When he walked into Billy's backyard, he glanced around at all the work going on and knew he should have stayed home. When Billy's dad saw Josh cutting through the neighbor's yard, heading toward them, he immediately stopped what he was doing and dashed off to the garage to get an extra pair of gloves.

"Glad you decided to come by, Josh," Billy's dad said, as he patted Josh on the back. "Billy told me this morning that you'd probably be over today. You did come over to help us with the fence, didn't you?"

"Oh, yes, sir. I ... I did. Is there anything I can help you with? I've never put a fence up before, so you'll have to show me what to do."

"That's fine, Josh, just fine. We appreciate that," Billy's dad answered, as he handed him the gloves. "Now, you see all those stakes in the ground around the yard? That's where all the fence posts will be going. Billy and I have already dug the first two holes, so you and Billy can start digging the rest. That should give me plenty of time to lay out the rest of these posts locations. Then we can start mixing the concrete. Thanks again for coming over, Josh. An extra hand makes all the difference when you're working on a big job like this one."

"I hope you know what you're doing, Billy," Josh said, after Billy's dad walked off. "I've never done this kind of stuff before, and my hands are still hurting from all that work we've been doing up at the cabin."

"Don't worry about it, Josh. I helped my dad put those other two posts in, and it's going to be a cinch!"

At first, digging the holes was boring work for Josh and Billy. But after they'd done a few, it became more of a game of speed than actual work. Each hole they dug took less and less time. By the time they got to the fifteenth one, it had taken them less than half the time it took to dig the first one. When they started digging the twenty-first hole, Billy's mom rang the dinner bell and walked over to the picnic table carrying a tray piled full of sandwiches. Billy's little sister, Suzy, followed close behind, carrying several bottles of pop.

The boys took off their gloves to sit down and eat and quickly discovered their hands were covered with blisters. They were so involved in the race to see how quickly they could dig the holes that they didn't feel the blisters forming beneath their gloves.

"It's good for you," Billy's dad, chuckled, as he looked down at their blistered hands. "A little hard work never hurt anyone. It'll make men out of you two."

But Billy's dad had no idea that the boys had already spent most of last weekend removing the roof from an old collapsed cabin, their hands were already sore and blistered, so hard work was nothing new to them.

Josh continued to help Billy and his dad with the fence over the next few days. By Saturday afternoon, everything was finished, even the painting. The only problem was, Josh and Billy were so worn out from building and painting the fence, that scavenging around the cabin up on the plateau was the furthest thing from their minds. On Sunday, after church was over and Josh had finished breakfast, his mother suggested that he should run over to Billy's to see if he'd like to go to the movies.

"Nah," Josh said, in his normal, no-I-don't-feel-like-it-today attitude.

"Oh, that's too bad. I think there's a pirate movie playing," she teased, peering at him from the corner of her eye.

"Really Mom …" Josh exclaimed, suddenly springing to life. "A pirate movie … what's the name of it?" He was so excited he couldn't think straight, since he and Billy loved pirate movies, just like every other boy their age.

"I'm not sure, but I know it's a new one. I think it's something about a Big Bearded Pirate or something like that."

"That's the one, Mom, but it's Black Beard the Pirate. That's the one I've been waiting to see. I saw the movie poster hanging outside the theater the last time Billy and I went by. I'll go get him right now!"

"You'd better hurry! It starts at twelve o'clock!" she shouted, as Josh darted out the front door.

Chapter Four

$\mathcal{W}$hen the movie ended, Josh and Billy relived the fight scene in Josh's back yard using a couple of branches as swords. Before they realized it, it was four o'clock, and Josh had to get inside for dinner. As Billy left to go home, they made a last minute decision to go back up to the plateau early the following day, which would be Monday, more than a week since their last visit to the site. They agreed to meet in front of Hammond's Hardware Store at six thirty sharp.

As Josh came around the corner of Coyne's Drug Store the next morning, he spotted Billy sitting on the bench in front of Hammond's Hardware Store, munching on potato chips out of the Charles Chips tin.

"Didn't you eat anything for breakfast this morning, Billy?" Josh asked, as he walked up and stood in front of the familiar red wagon.

"Nah ... didn't have time. I got up late, and I thought you'd be waiting for me again, so I just grabbed a few things and ran down here as quickly as I could."

After seeing that pirate movie the day before, the boys couldn't wait to get back up to the site to continue searching for more treasures. Walking toward the old lady's house the boys watched as she watered plants around her front porch. The squeaky wheels on Billy's wagon seemed loud enough to wake up the whole neighborhood, but she didn't seem to acknowledge that they were even there at all, at least not until they got right in front her house.

"Good morning boys," she said with a big smile on her face. "You be careful up in those woods today."

"Yes ma'am," the boys replied, a bit bewildered at her behavior as they sped up their pace toward the log bridge.

"Wow!" Josh commented. "She was actually nice that time."

"Yup," Billy said, with an authoritarian tone. "Just like my grand-mother. Don't you remember me telling you about her last week! It's like, one day she's completely normal, and the next, she doesn't even know who I am. Usually on the days when she doesn't remember me, she's a little mean. That old lady acts the same way. Remember that time last year when she yelled at us? Then last week she wasn't as bad, but then today, wow, she was as nice as could be. I guess I just don't understand old people."

They started to cross the old log bridge, when an owl suddenly let out several loud hooting sounds. It nearly scared the daylights out of them. Billy paused for a moment as he looked up and scanned the treetops in search of the owl, and then suddenly spotted him perched high on a branch, as though he were guarding the bridge.

"I think he's sleeping," Billy whispered, walking backwards across the bridge.

Josh continued staring up at the owl until Billy reached the other side of the log bridge; then he took off running across the bridge until he passed Billy on the other side. He figured that if the owl was going to fly down after him, Billy was going to get attacked first.

"Josh, what are you doing? I already told you he was sleeping. That's what owls do in the daytime. They're not going to swoop down from their perch and chase after us, if that's what you're thinking. It's not in their nature. My teacher, Mrs. Fox, said that owls only go after things like mice, small birds, and a limited variety of small bugs and insects ... not people."

"I know," Josh nervously responded, as he continued to walk up the hill backwards, keeping a keen eye on the owl. "It just gives me the willies the way it keeps staring down at me."

"That owl is *sleeping*, Josh. Believe me you've got nothing to worry about."

When they reached the cabin site, everything appeared to be exactly the same as when they left eight days earlier. Billy parked the wagon next to the rock wall so they would have easy access to all their supplies. They stepped over the rock wall and noticed that the rain had washed away some of the loose dirt from the floor around the bed.

"Josh, what's that sticking out of the floor over by the bed? That wasn't there the last time we were here."

"I don't know," Josh reflected, moving over to that corner. "It feels like a burlap bag," he said. He used the claw end of his hammer to dig the dirt away from their new discovery.

After countless minutes of digging and sifting through the dirt, Billy pulled out an oversized bundle of burlap shaped like a football. The bundle was several layers thick and secured with numerous wraps of twine, which were mostly disintegrated. They carefully used the claw of their hammers to knock off the clumps of dirt from the burlap.

Once they were finished unwinding layer after layer, they finally removed the last piece of burlap. Although this wasn't quite what they expected to find, they still considered it another piece of treasure. Josh didn't have any idea what it was, but Billy knew right off. They were carving tools; a complete set, much like his grandfathers, but this wasn't your everyday ordinary set. This was top of the line, the kind only a professional wood carver would use. The tools were also in surprisingly good shape for having been buried in the ground. Whoever put them in that hole knew how to preserve them, because they were completely covered in a thick coat of oil to keep them from rusting. There was also a large sand stone packed within another burlap bag buried beneath the tools. Billy wiped the oil off one of the carving tools and held the piece up to the light.

"Look at this, Josh. The letter *W,* just like what was carved into the footboard."

Every tool Billy picked up had the same *W* carved into the bottom of the handle.

"Looks like this Wendell fellow carved his initial into everything he owned," Billy said, as he examined the rest of the tools. "My grandfather has a set sort of like this one on his workbench down in his cellar, but they're not quite as fancy as these."

"What's your grandfather doing with carving tools?"

"He used to make furniture when he wasn't working at the lumber mill. It was his hobby. He made that big shelf that sits in the corner of my room. My dad said he was one of the best in town, until he got that arthritis."

"How'd he get that?"

"Don't know. My dad said that he carved so much stuff during his lifetime that his hands just starting hurting to the point where they wouldn't work right anymore. He even has a hard time holding onto a fork while he's eating. Every time he and my grandma come over for dinner, he blames me for knocking his fork out of his hand. He likes to play jokes a lot. The last time I went down to my grandpa's cellar, his carving tools were still sitting on his old workbench, covered with dust. I don't think he goes down there much anymore."

"What are we going to do with them?" Josh asked.

"I guess we'll just wrap them back up and take them home. I'll hide them in that old green cabinet under the cellar stairs, at least until we can figure out what to do with them. Nobody ever looks under there anyway."

While Billy loaded the burlap sack into the wagon, Josh continued ripping the rest of the roof apart that still covered up more than half of the dirt floor. By nine o'clock in the morning, the temperature felt like a hundred degrees. There was almost no breeze blowing through the trees, and there was hardly any shade where the boys were working. Billy walked over to the wagon and opened up his second bottle of pop.

"We're going to have to make a trip down to the creek pretty soon," Billy said, lifting the pop bottle to take the last swig. "There isn't anything else left to drink!"

"I'd like to go down there just to take a dip in the water to cool off," Josh remarked, as he heaved a few more boards onto the pile. "I wonder what else is buried under all this," he continued, changing the subject and studying the exposed area of the dirt floor. "It seems like if he buried his pants and his carving tools, he probably would have buried a whole lot more. Let's hurry up and get the rest of the roof cleared away, so we can start digging up this dirt floor. I'll bet there's stuff buried all over this place."

They spent another three hours clearing the rest of the roof away, at which point they were able to get a better look at the sidewalls that had been buried underneath. The walls were surprisingly intact, with only the exposed ends showing any signs of rotted wood. After lifting one end to check how heavy the wall was, Billy decided that he and Josh could easily lift and push the partition over the rock wall. His plan worked perfectly.

The next morning, before Billy left the house, he threw a broom, two shovels, and a pick into the wagon so he and Josh could start digging up the dirt floor.

"Just one second there, young man!" Billy's father shouted, stepping off the front porch where he'd been watching Billy pull the wagon full of his yard tools down the driveway and onto the sidewalk. "Where do you think you're going with my new shovel?"

Billy tried desperately to come up with a quick answer as to why he was taking all this stuff up to the plateau. His father removed his new shovel from the wagon and walked back into the garage.

"Here!" his father yelled, as he came strolling back down the driveway. "Take this old shovel. I just bought that other one last week, so if you don't mind; I'd like to keep it in one piece for a while. And make sure you're careful with that pick! If your mom knew you were using that, she'd have a conniption. You go on and run along now. Just make sure you and Josh stay out of trouble."

"Thanks, Dad. Josh and I are just doing some digging up in the woods. We can't get into any trouble doing that!"

Billy brought along some change this time to buy a couple bottles of pop from the machine in front of the hardware store. He'd heard the weatherman on the radio predicting that the temperature would be even hotter today than it was yesterday.

"Morning, Billy," Josh said, as he plopped down on the bench in front of the hardware store, holding one of his nice, cool, freshly opened bottles of pop.

"How long have you been waiting?" Billy asked, as he pulled a nickel out of his pocket and pushed it into the pop machine's coin slot. "I thought I'd be waiting for you today."

"I just got here a few minutes ago," Josh said, taking another swig.

"Hey, you brought a water cooler. Nice going, Josh."

"It's Kool-Aid. My mom made it this morning. When I got home yesterday, I told her we ran out of pop and ended up drinking water out of the creek. She didn't think that was too sanitary and she kind of felt sorry for us. Anyway, she got up early this morning and made us this Kool-Aid and some sandwiches too."

"Billy, do your parents ever ask you what you've been doing up in the woods?"

"At first my mom did. I just told her we were building a fort. I guess she thinks we're still working on it because she doesn't ask me anymore."

"Yeah, I told my parents the same thing. They didn't seem to care either," Josh replied. "Well, you ready, Billy? Today might be our lucky day."

"You bet I am. Brought us two shovels and a pick today, now we'll be able to start digging up that dirt floor to see what else Wendell might have buried."

When they reached the site and parked the wagon, Billy noticed that the big pile of wet moldy wood that they had pulled off the roof had completely dried over night. The mold was actually starting to crack and break off. In fact, the hot weather was drying everything out. Even the leaves were dying and falling from the trees, littering the dirt floor. Billy grabbed the broom out of the wagon and started sweeping them up in a pile, while Josh pulled out the pick and started chopping up the floor.

During the next few weeks, all they dug up were a few more pieces of clothing, some old cooking utensils, two chipped plates, and a wooden ruler. At that point, Josh and Billy began having second thoughts about all the digging they were doing and decided to stop. The experience hadn't exactly turned out to be the treasure hunt they had hoped for, especially after all their time and hard work. In fact, the closest thing to a piece of treasure they'd found was an old wooden ruler with a brass edge bearing the same carving of a *W*.

Chapter Five

$\mathcal{S}$ eptember rolled around with unbelievable speed, and school had started. The summer had promised to be the most exciting one ever for Billy and Josh, once they found that old cabin. But after wasting most of their vacation digging for buried treasure they never found, all they had to show for their efforts was major disappointment.

On his first day as a seventh-grader, Josh sat down at the back of his classroom, half listening to what his teacher expected of everyone during the school year. Without being able to stop himself, he began daydreaming about the cabin on the plateau. He thought back to that first day when he and Billy came down from the plateau and passed by the old lady's house. She stopped them to ask if they'd found Wendell's gold chain. "*What did she mean ... what did she mean, did you find Wendell's gold chain?*" He kept repeating this question to himself, trying to make some sense out of the old lady's words. "*What was the big deal with that gold chain,*" he thought. "*Why is it that she can remember that chain but not remember that she told us we couldn't go up to her side of the plateau in the first place. And who was this Wendell fellow?*"

After Josh left his last class of the day, he met up with Billy in the hallway for their walk home together. On their way, Josh mentioned to Billy that he'd been thinking about Wendell and what the old lady had said to them. Billy thought this was weird, because for the last few days, he'd been thinking about the same thing. As they continued discussing the situation, they were a little confused as to what they should do next. At first they thought about going back to talk to the old lady. But she was too unpredictable, and they were a little paranoid about asking her. Billy suggested they go down to the county library and ask Mrs. Jenkins. She knew just about everyone in town. So, they made a quick detour and headed down Maple Street to the library.

As they walked into the building, Mrs. Jenkins was standing at the front desk, stamping a large stack of those checkout cards that slip inside the books' front covers. The boys strolled up to the large, round, wooden desk. She glanced down at them through the top of her reading glasses, without missing a beat of what she was doing. Suddenly, she put down the stamp and moved the pile of cards to one side.

"Well, hello there, boys," she said. "Now, Josh and Billy, I haven't seen you two in here in a month of Sundays. What can I help you with?"

"Mrs. Jenkins, Billy and I were wondering if you know anyone from around town by the name of Wendell."

"Wendell ... Wendell," Mrs. Jenkins repeated, folding her arms and tapping on her chin with her index finger. "No ... no, I don't recall ever knowing *anyone* with a name like that. Maybe if you could describe him to me, I would remember his face."

"We don't know what he looks like," Billy replied. "The old lady that lives down at the end of the dirt road told us about him. We think he used to live in the old broken-down cabin up on the plateau."

"Gee, I'm sorry, boys. I don't think I'll be able to help you. But I'll be sure to ask around! If he ever lived in these parts, someone in this town must have known him."

Josh thanked her politely, and then he and Billy left the building.

The next few days at school seemed to drag on, as the boys began making plans to go back up to the plateau early Saturday morning. They'd decided to do some more digging along the rock wall and pull the rest of the wood away from the front porch area to see if anything was buried there.

By ten o'clock Saturday morning, they had already cleared away a large portion of wood that exposed the ground under the front porch. It was about ten-thirty when Josh removed the last board. After he tossed the board in the pile, he took one step over the rock wall to where Billy was digging up more of the floor and noticed something strange. There was something different about how the rocks were secured in place. Josh glanced around at the other three rock walls and noticed they were firmly set in place with concrete. But this group of rocks was different. Bending down to take a closer look, Josh noticed several thin wooden wedges shoved in around more than thirty of the rocks, keeping them tightly in place.

"Billy, you've got to come over here and take a look at this."

"What?" Billy replied, as he walked over and stood next to Josh.

"Billy, I think there's something behind this wall; look at all these wooden wedges. I think they're holding all these rocks in place."

They knelt down and began to examine the wedges. The wooden wedges were definitely there for a purpose; no other area of the rock wall had any wedges. Suddenly, Billy grabbed hold of one and slowly pulled it out. One of the rocks moved about a quarter inch, but was still secured within the wall by three wedges. But as soon as Josh pulled out two of the three about ten rocks came tumbling down from the wall, narrowly missing their feet, leaving a one foot square hole. Billy immediately jumped up and ran to the wagon to get the flashlight. When he shined it into the dark hole, he was shocked by what he saw.

"It's a treasure chest, Josh! We found it! A real life treasure chest! It's the buried treasure, Josh, just like the one we saw in that pirate movie. This is what we've been looking for!"

"Let *me* take a look!" Josh replied, anxious to see for himself and snatching the light from Billy's hand. "It *is*! It really *is* a treasure chest!"

With the flashlight still in his hand, Josh pulled out the other wedges and the entire wall tumbled down. Then the boys starting grabbing and throwing the rocks clear of the area so they would have room to pull out the chest. Now that the front of the chest was fully exposed, they sat down and just stared at what they'd unearthed. Bigger than anything they'd expected to find, it was roughly the size of a laundry basket and was definitely made of wood, but heavily covered with something black. Billy rapped on the side to see if he could tell whether the coffer was empty or full.

"It looks like that black stuff people put on their roofs," Billy declared.

"That's called *tar*, Billy." Josh said in a sarcastic voice.

"I *know* what it is! I just couldn't think of the word for a second. My dad and I had to use this stuff to patch up my grandpa's roof last spring to stop the rain from leaking through. It's messy stuff, but it works great. Maybe that's why Wendell put tar all over this chest, so it'd stay dry inside."

Josh grabbed onto one of the large leather straps that was attached to the front face of the chest and gave it a tug. "It won't budge," he moaned, continuing to pull until his face started turning red.

The handle was plenty big enough for two hands, so Billy grabbed hold and they both began pulling. After a few good tugs, they were finally able to break it free from its rocky tomb and pulled it out onto the dirt floor. Except for the hinges and the opening around the lid, the whole chest was covered with tar. There were two large padlocks fastened on the front. The padlocks were antiques and unlike anything they'd ever seen before, they were oval shaped and heavily adorned with fancy designs, but slightly obscured by the rust. There wasn't anything fancy about the chest, though; no markings or large **W** for Wendell ... just a big old tar-covered chest.

They stood up and walked around the chest for several minutes, trying to figure out how to get into it. Billy was sure it would be full of stolen money from some long ago train robbery, or maybe some loot from one of the banks in town. Josh was holding out for rubies and diamonds, or a chest full of gold coins from an old pirate ship. For the next few minutes, they loaded the heavy chest up onto Billy's wagon. Then they agreed that Billy's garage would be the best place to go so they could use his dad's hacksaw to remove the locks.

As they pulled the wagon, with the tar-covered chest, down the sidewalk through downtown, everyone stopped and stared. Every time someone asked them what they had in the box, they shied away and started to walk faster. It wasn't long before they began running through town. Mr. Hammond stood in front of his hardware store, leaning on his broom, just smiling and shaking his head as he watched the boys dodging people on the sidewalk across the street. He wasn't a bit *curious* about what they had in the chest. He just got a kick out of seeing all the people lunge out of the way trying to avoid getting run over.

When they finally arrived at Billy's house, the garage door was open and there was no car in sight.

"Josh, hurry up and take the wagon around to the back of the garage. I'll get my dad's hacksaw."

After several failed attempts at sawing through the padlocks, the boys tried thinking up another way to get the locks off.

"A sledgehammer," Billy shouted. "I'll go get my dad's sledge hammer. That'll get those locks off!"

Billy hurried back into the garage and returned with the big sledgehammer. After a few practice swings, he let go with a powerful whack at the first padlock, which broke completely in half. The only thing remaining was the half-ring portion dangling at the latch.

"Wow!" Josh declared, as he pulled the ring from the latch and picked the broken lock up off the ground. "Good hit, Billy! Do you think you can do that to the other one?"

"Not sure, but I'll give it a try."

After about eight swings and several misses, the second lock finally broke loose and Josh quickly removed the busted pieces. They glanced over at each other as if to say, "Good luck and I hope you find what you wished for," and then they each grabbed onto a latch and lifted with all their might to break the lid free.

Inside the chest, neatly stacked and numbered in sequential order by years, were forty-four hard-covered books. Each book was exactly the same size, dark green in color, with gold and red trim. The books ranged in years from 1896 to 1940.

The boys just stood motionless, staring down into the chest. There was no gold, no money, no diamonds or even rubies … just some very old worthless books.

"I can't believe this!" Billy said in anger. "All that time up there, most of our summer vacation, all for a bunch of worthless books. What now Josh? What are we supposed to do with all these books?"

Josh gave a slight tug and brought the lid crashing down. "Right this minute, I really don't care. I'm too disappointed."

After complaining about all the time they'd wasted digging for buried treasure that never materialized, they went into Billy's house to get something to drink.

While Josh sat Indian style on the floor in Billy's room, he rested his head against the wall and stared up at the ceiling. Even though Billy continued to go on and on about the lack of finding any real treasure, Josh wasn't listening. All he could think about was the chest full of books. "*What were they, and why would someone bury them in the rocks? What were they trying to hide?*" After another ten minutes, Josh stood up and told Billy he had to be getting home. When he left Billy's house, he snuck around to the back of the garage and quietly opened the lid to the chest. Josh reached in and grabbed a bunch of books, ten to be exact, years 1896 through 1905. He quietly closed the lid, and with five books tucked under each arm, he darted around the garage to the sidewalk and raced home.

Chapter Six

That night after Josh finished dinner, he raced up to his bedroom, grabbed the book dated 1896, that was neatly arranged in order along with the other nine books on the shelf, and sat on the edge of his bed. Before he opened the front cover he slowly ran his fingers over the date and the gold and red trim along the spine of the binding. A smidgen of gold rubbed off on his index finger. *"That looks like real gold,"* he whispered, as he held his finger up toward the ceiling light to admire the sparkle.

Josh carefully opened the front cover and got his first glimpse of the strange handwriting. The font was unlike anything he had ever seen before, but similar to the old English style of writing you would normally see on an old Charles Dickens' book cover. The pages were lightly browned on the edges but otherwise in excellent condition. As Josh began reading, he quickly realized that this was more than just a mere book, it was a journal. He then read:

"It's been three weeks since I fell from the sleigh. The soft pine branches broke my fall and saved my life, but my gold chain that was connected to my watch has gone missing, and the watch has now stopped ticking. I took shelter in an old abandoned cabin that was close by. The cabin is located on a plateau within a couple miles of a small town called Whispering Pines. It's an old logging town with at least two dozen furniture factories. There is one place in

particular that is managed by a nice gentleman who answers to the name of Rush. I believe that's only his nickname, though. After I used his tools to carve him a squirrel, he was kind enough to give me a job and started me off at two dollars a day. The way I understand it, that's pretty good wages these days. He must really like squirrels to have started me off that high. I'm currently carving fancy table legs. They seem to think a ten hour work day is long enough, so that gives me plenty of time to search for my gold chain and to journal my day's activities. Also, I've met a very nice girl by the name of Millie. Her folks own the land and the cabin where I'm staying. They live in a small house at the base of the plateau."

Josh closed the book and fell back on his bed. He'd never read anything like this before. He sat back up and read it again. The falling from the sleigh part was confusing, but he quickly guessed that Millie had to be the old lady's name.

For the next few days, Josh hid from Billy the fact that he had taken the journals out of the chest. He knew that Billy was still upset that the chest they found wasn't full of the treasure they'd both wished for. Josh also wanted to spend more time reading before telling Billy what the journals were about.

Reading through the journals was taking forever; not only was the fancy lettering hard to read, the words were written so close together that they were difficult to decipher. This made the whole reading process very slow and tedious.

By the end of the first week, Josh had finally read through most of the first journal and was ready to break the news to Billy. Josh was just about to ring the front door bell when he noticed Billy walking up the driveway with a handful of boards.

"Hey, Billy," Josh shouted.

"Hi, Josh. Come here and open the gate for me so I can set these boards out by the tree house."

While Billy climbed up the ladder to the tree house, Josh broke the news to him about reading the first journal as he handed him up some boards.

"I knew you couldn't resist," Billy said, laughing. "I was surprised when you didn't make me help you load all those books in the wagon that day we found them and take them over to your house. So, who wrote them?"

"Wendell," Josh answered. "He fell out of a … Santa's sleigh and landed in a giant pine tree back in 1896 over by that cabin we found."

"Santa's sleigh," Billy repeated, as he stopped what he was doing and looked down at Josh.

"Are you telling me that he actually fell out of Santa Claus's sleigh? How is that possible? So you're telling me that all those books are about Santa Claus and elves and all that fairy tale stuff?"

"Yup, that's exactly what Wendell wrote about in his first journal," Josh said, as he elaborated to Billy on more of what he'd read. After a while Billy started to ask questions as he, too, was being drawn into the realism and excitement of the story.

For the next few weeks or so, Josh and Billy went to school, worked on each other's tree houses, and made five bucks each by helping Jimmy Smith pick the Indian corn up on the plateau. They also spent numerous hours at Josh's house reading through Wendell's journals. Yes, even Billy began reading. It was almost like searching for lost treasure again, except this time it was by research through Wendell's journals. They also made a couple trips back to Billy's house to gather the remaining journals and stacked them neatly, in order by year, on Josh's book shelf.

During the second week in October, while Billy's parents were out in the backyard raking up the leaves, Billy's mom Claire spotted the chest out of the corner of her eye.

"Bob," said Claire, as she pointed towards the garage, "where did that old trunk come from?"

"I don't know. I've never seen it before. Billy must have dragged it home from one of his scrounging adventures. Maybe he and Josh have plans for it."

But, Billy's mom was too curious to let it go, and she walked up to the trunk and lifted the lid to see what was inside.

"It's empty," Claire said. "Now where on earth would Billy have found a chest like this? The outside is all sealed up with this tar, but the inside is spotless. You don't suppose there was something in here, do you?" Claire questioned, as she looked at Bob.

"I think you missed your calling, Claire," Bob said jokingly. "You should have been a private eye instead of a nurse, but I think you're right about the tar. It appears that it was intentionally plastered onto this trunk to seal it up and protect whatever may have been kept inside."

As Bob lowered the lid he noticed the two broken locks lying in the weeds next to the chest.

"Yup," Bob said, as he picked up one of the locks and held it up for Claire to see. "Looks like Billy may have some explaining to do."

Twenty minutes later Billy and Josh came strolling in through the back yard gate.

When Claire and Bob heard the gate shut they stopped raking leaves and waited for the boys to get closer.

"Hi, Mom and Dad," Billy said, as he and Josh continued on their way toward the back door.

"One second there, boys," Claire demanded. "Do you two know where this old trunk came from?" as she walked toward the back of the garage.

Josh and Billy looked at each other to see who was going to answer the question.

"Um ..." Billy stammered. "Josh and I found it up on the plateau behind the old lady's house."

"Okay," Claire said. "And was there anything inside this chest?"

"Yes, ma'am," Billy answered. "It was...."

"It was full of old journals, Mrs. Phillips," Josh blurted out. "Forty-four volumes to be exact; they belong to a fellow by the name of Wendell."

Claire and Bob, not knowing quite what to say, stood in silence for a moment.

"Who's Wendell?" Bob asked.

"We don't know," Billy answered. "The old lady mentioned his name once and ..."

"Slow down boys," Claire interrupted, "this is getting a little confusing."

"Why don't you just start from the beginning and tell us the whole story?"

"Well," Billy said, as he slowly began to tell his version of the story, "on that last day of school before summer vacation, Josh and I took the long way home ... you know, up through the plateau and down the old lady's road. Anyway, we started chasing these rabbits, and they led us to the old broken down cabin on the old lady's side of the plateau. And when we came down from the plateau and walked past the old lady's house, she stopped us and asked if we had found Wendell's gold chain. That's when we got the idea to go back up there to start digging around. That's where we spent most of our summer. We found a burlap bag full of old woodcarving tools buried in the dirt floor of the cabin, and they all had a **W** carved in the handles. Plus, there's a busted up bed that also had the initial **W** carved in it. You see, it all belongs to Wendell!"

Both Bob and Claire just looked at the boys and shook their heads. They'd never heard such a story, and neither one of them had ever heard of anyone by the name of Wendell. They also didn't realize that someone had once lived in a cabin up on the plateau. The boys continued on with their story telling them everything, from chasing the rabbit down the ravine, to finding the collapsed cabin, to the talks they had with the old lady.

"And what about you, Josh," Claire said. "I'm guessing you haven't mentioned any of this to your parents either, have you?"

"No ma'am, you and Mr. Phillips are the only ones besides Billy and I that know anything about this ... except for the old lady. Actually, I think her name is Millie. Wendell talks about her in his first journal."

"Oh, so the old lady ... I mean Millie, she knows that you have these journals?" Claire inquired.

"Well ..." Billy paused, "no, not exactly. She doesn't know anything about the journals; we never told her that we took them. She only thinks that we've been up there searching around for Wendell's gold chain. But I guess she's okay with that, she did give us permission, honest."

Claire told the boys that she needed to talk to Josh's mom, and she turned around and walked into the house to phone her. She wanted to hear what Kate had to say about all this. After all, Kate was Claire's co-worker down at the nursing home and her best friend; they never kept any secrets from each other.

After a fifteen minute conversation in which Claire related to Kate everything the boys had told her, Kate said to send Josh home so she could have a talk with him. Kate knew Josh was a good honest boy and was disappointed that he didn't come and talk to her first.

An hour later, after Kate and Josh had their talk, she called Claire back and they decided that tomorrow after church they would take the boys and drive down to Millie's house. They were counting on Millie to know the whereabouts of Wendell so they could return his journals.

That next day, they drove through town and made their first left onto the dirt road that led to Millie's house. When the car crept to a stop in front of the house, they all climbed out and walked towards the front steps. Suddenly, Millie opened the screen door and shuffled her way over to the rocking chair and sat down. Most of the cats were inside, but the few that were on the porch happily greeted them.

"Can I help you folks with something?" she snapped.

"Yes, ma'am, you can," Kate spoke. "My son, Josh, here, and his friend, Billy, have been spending a lot of time lately up at that old cabin on the plateau behind your house, and they dug up an old trunk full of journals. They said they belong to someone by the name of Wendell. Do you know where we can find him? We'd like to return his journals."

Millie settled back in her chair and began rocking. After a few moments of silence, she stopped and leaned forward on her cane to look into the boys' eyes.

"Did you boys find Wendell's gold chain up there yet?" she inquired. "Can't wait to see the look on his face when he sees that gold chain again ..."

"Ma'am," Billy's mom interrupted, "they only found some old journals. There was no gold chain. If you would, could you please just tell us where we can find Wendell, and then we'll just be on our way."

Millie smiled and leaned back in her chair, continuing to rock again, as if no one were even there.

Billy grabbed his mother's arm to get her attention. "Mom," he whispered, "she won't answer you anymore. She does this all the time. She's already forgotten who we are, just like grandma does. She'll just sit there for a while and mumble about Wendell and his gold chain."

That night, while Josh was in his bedroom reading the second year of Wendell's journals, his mother walked in and sat down on his bed.

"Have you read anything in those journals yet about where Wendell may have gone?" Kate asked, as Josh stopped reading and looked over at her.

"Not yet. These journals are really hard to read, Mom. Wendell wrote down everything in here. Every little thing that happened during the day he wrote in these journals. And if the amount of words isn't overwhelming enough, he wrote them so close together it takes forever to read."

Josh handed his mother the journal and she quickly realized what he was talking about.

"I see your point, Josh. This would be difficult for anyone to read. Maybe there was a reason Wendell wrote it like this. But in any case, we have to find out where we can find him so we can do the right thing and return these journals to him. You do understand that, don't you Josh?"

"Yeah, Mom, but if we have to read through all these journals to find out where he is, Billy and I are going to need some help."

Before Kate left Josh's room, she went over to the bookshelf, gazed over all the other journals and pulled out the one dated 1896. As she walked past the bed, Josh thanked her, in advance, for helping.

Kate walked down stairs, into the living room, plopped down into her favorite chair, and began reading.

"I thought you and the boys were going to give those books back to their rightful owner?" John said, as he dropped one corner of the newspaper he was reading to look at Kate from across the room.

"This isn't going to be quite that easy, John. It turns out that all those journals the boys found belong to a gentleman by the name of Wendell, whom we can't seem to locate at the moment. I thought if I read through this first journal I could maybe find some clues to his whereabouts or maybe some names of friends or family."

"Well, good luck with that," John smirked, as he resumed reading his newspaper.

Chapter Seven

*O*nce Kate began reading Wendell's first journal, she couldn't put it down. Finally, around one o'clock in the morning, after reading for several hours, her eyes grew heavy and she started to nod off. A few moments later, her hands relaxed and the journal, which she was holding in her right hand, fell with a thump onto the soft carpeted floor. But Kate was sleeping and didn't hear a thing.

As morning approached and daylight slowly crept through the front window and across the room, Kate opened her eyes and began to stretch. Then she leaned over the right arm of the chair and picked up the journal. This wasn't the first time she'd fallen asleep in her chair while reading, but it was the first time she slept there all night.

"Good morning," John whispered, as he walked down the stairs and into the living room. "I thought you'd end up staying down here all night. You were so engrossed in that journal last night that you never even answered me when I told you I was going to bed."

"Oh, I'm sorry," she apologized, stretching and yawning again. "Once I started, I couldn't put it down. I think it must have put me in some kind of a trance. Then while I slept, I had the strangest dream about one of Santa's elves falling out of his sleigh and landing in a ... a giant pine tree. Wait! That ... that wasn't a dream! That's what I read in this journal. Wendell is the one I dreamed about. I've never remembered a dream so clearly before. I could probably tell you every little detail about it."

"So, what are you saying, Kate? That this Wendell fellow is one of Santa's elves?"

"No. Well ... yes ... Oh, I don't know. This ... this journal is so ... so real. When I was reading it, I felt like I was there, really there. I've never read anything like this before. It's like ... *the real thing.* He also mentioned that gold chain the boys were talking about. He wrote that he lost it when he fell out of Santa's sleigh. This book is written like a fantasy that took place fifty-six years ago. So I doubt very much if Wendell is still around."

"Kate, maybe these are just stories. Why would you ever think they're anything more than that?"

"They're all dated, John. Why on earth would anyone write a fantasy story over a forty-four year period?"

"Good point; that *is* a long time. But just the same Kate, it's just a *story.* You know for yourself, that Christmas, and Santa with all his elves, are just make believe. They're not *real.* It's only fantasy, Kate ... it's just a story."

Kate sat still, collecting her thoughts for a moment before she walked up to Josh's room to return the journal. When she walked back downstairs, John was in the kitchen making coffee.

"You're right," Kate said, as she strolled into the kitchen and wrapped her arms around John. "I guess I was just caught up in the story. It was so real and so well written that it actually pulled you in and made you a believer ... like magic. And I wasn't even half way through when I dozed off."

"Well," John began, "I think since the boys are the ones responsible for taking the journals in the first place, they should find the person who owns them ... this, Wendell fellow."

Kate paused for a moment. "You're probably right, John." Kate said, with clenched teeth, "Claire and I will make sure they do just that."

While Kate was getting ready to go to work, she thought about what Josh had said to her last night when she walked past him carrying Wendell's first journal. *"Thanks in advance for helping Mom."*

"I can't just stand around doing nothing. I have to help the boys. Claire and I will help the boys," Kate whispered to herself.

Kate and Claire had a long history: they'd grown up together in the same neighborhood, graduated high school and college together, married within two months of each other, and gave birth to baby boys only thirty days apart, with Josh being the oldest. They were also hired on the same day at the nursing home. Everyone that knew them joked that they must have been twins who were separated at birth.

When Kate arrived at work that morning, she revealed to Claire what she had read so far in Wendell's first journal. The same journal the boys had already read. Claire laughed at first, certain that Kate was joking, but after hearing the whole story explained to her, she was in awe. Claire too, had never heard such a story. So from that moment on, the girls were on a mission to help the boys. One way or another, and without their husbands finding out, the girls were going to do what they could to assist the boys in locating Wendell. This would be their Christmas present to themselves; a good deed to finish out the year.

In the mean time, the boys were conjuring up their own plan to rally for help. Maybe they could recruit their friends from school. Josh didn't have any really close friends except Billy, but knew of several kids at school who would enjoy helping them read through all the journals. And Billy, even though he himself wasn't an avid reader, could coax a few of *his* friends, who did enjoy reading, to help as well.

The plan was set and the kids from school who Josh and Billy chose to help were invited to Josh's house after school to listen to what the boys needed. The boys decided to only discuss working on a special project together and didn't mention anything about Wendell or his journals. They didn't want to scare anyone away.

Not long after school was out, seven kids from school sat in Josh's living room, ready to listen to what the boys had to say. Billy, being the more outgoing, of the two, started to tell the story from the beginning. Josh sat and listened carefully to make sure he didn't leave out any details. But as Billy was closing in on the end of the story, Josh glanced around the room and noticed some of the kids yawning and fidgeting as if they weren't interested.

"Come on, Billy," Rusty, blurted out. "Are you serious? Just because you and Josh found some old wood carvings and stuff, you want us to help you find this Wendell fellow who the old lady said *used to* live up there in a cabin? What kind of fun is that?"

"That's not the whole story, Rusty," Josh interjected, fearing that everyone was going to start running for the front door. "Wait here a second; I have something to show you guys."

Josh ran upstairs to his room and grabbed several volumes of Wendell's journals from his shelf.

"This is what we need help with," Josh said, as he plopped himself down on the floor and spread the journals out in front of him. "Billy and I found these inside a big chest buried within a stone wall up at the cabin. There are forty-four of these journals all together. We've read through the first volume, but because of Wendell's fancy handwriting, it's difficult to read, and it's going to take Billy and me forever to read through them. All we need is for you guys to help us find enough information in these journals to either lead us to Wendell, a friend or a family member so we can return all the journals."

"That doesn't seem too hard," Christine said. "So all you want us to do is help you read?"

"Yeah," Josh answered.

"If that's all there is to it, count me in," Melissa said, as she reached for one of the journals.

"Wait," Josh snapped, as he snatched up all the journals. "I mean ... hold on. There ... there's just one more thing I need to mention. "Wendell ... he ... he's an elf. At least we think he's an elf. Wait, listen to this," as Josh picked up the first journal and read aloud the first part about when Wendell fell out of Santa's sleigh.

The seven kids quietly looked around at each other. They didn't know how to react to this kind of news. None of them believed in Santa Claus anymore.

"What about the other forty-three journals?" Patty questioned. "What are those about?"

"Forty-four years of his life here in this town, I guess," Josh answered.

"OK," Greg said, breaking the silence. "I don't know who this Wendell person is, but maybe he's had a real exciting life. We might learn something. Hey, maybe he wrote a lot of secrets in there that he never told anyone."

Everyone in the room agreed with Greg, even Rusty. Josh also made everyone promise to keep this a secret, just between the group for now. If word of this got out to all the other kids in school, they would never hear the end of it. They'd be branded for life as the kids who *still* believed in Santa Claus.

They collectively decided to meet each afternoon for one hour immediately after school at Josh's house and then a couple hours on Saturday and Sunday. The goal was to find some pertinent information about Wendell, any information.

Kate and Claire sat in the break room during their lunch hour and began strategizing a plan where they could work incognito so that neither the boys nor their husbands would find out what they were up to.

"So, Kate, what do you suggest we do first?" Claire asked.

"Well ..." Kate paused, as she was already in the process of jotting down some notes. "Why don't we start with what we know so far like his name? We already know his name is Wendell, he's lived in this town since 1896, and he was good friends with Millie."

"That's a good start, Kate. So, since he lived and worked in this town for a considerable amount of time, he must have shopped, and maybe even attended one of the church's here."

"That's right, Claire, so it only seems logical that a certain percentage of the elderly folks in town must have known Wendell."

"What about the county courthouse?" Claire suggested. "If he worked somewhere here in town, he must have paid taxes or something where we could find some kind of records on him."

Kate continued eating her lunch, trying to think of ideas and writing notes down at the same time. Kate and Claire worked well together, they always have. This project was going to be exciting for them, just like old times.

"Wait a second," Claire blurted out. "Matilda used to work part time down at the courthouse."

"Matilda! Our, Matilda?" Kate questioned.

"Yup, during college she worked as a clerk in the county records office. That's how she paid part of her way through nursing school."

"Then she might still know some of the people that work down there," Kate added, the excitement building up in her voice. "After all, she's only been out of school for about five years. They'd probably let her search through any files she wanted to. Like you said, Claire, there must be some old records on him there: employment, taxes, maybe even a military record."

First thing Tuesday morning, Kate and Claire sat in the nurse's lounge drinking coffee and sharing some strategy while they waited patiently for Matilda to arrive. When Matilda finally walked through the doorway, she nearly jumped when the girls shouted "good morning, Matilda" in unison. Then they continued to watch her as she walked over to get some coffee.

"Okay, you two," Matilda said, as she picked up the coffee pot and turned around to face the girls. "What's with the loud good morning and the staring me down; what are you two up to?"

"We need to ask you a favor," Claire blurted out, as she looked over at Kate as if seeking approval.

"Ok, what do you need?"

"Well," Kate began, "to make a long story short we're trying to locate someone and we need you to use your contacts down at the county records office."

"Who are you looking for? Maybe *I* know this person?"

"A man by the name of Wendell," Kate answered. "Just Wendell, we don't know his last name."

While Matilda thought about it she took a sip of coffee. "No ... I'm drawing a blank here. I'm pretty sure I've never heard that name before, at least not in this town. That's an unusual name, I'm quite certain I'd remember that one. How soon would you need this information? Because my friend April still works down there in the records department. I'm sure she wouldn't have a problem letting us come down there to do a little *harmless* research."

"That would be fantastic," Kate smiled. "We would like to start as soon as possible, if you don't mind."

Later that day during lunch, Matilda informed Kate and Claire that she had talked to her friend April, over at the county clerk's office, and she said it would be fine for them to come by tomorrow after work to begin their research.

The next day after work, Kate and Claire met Matilda at the courthouse where her friend April was waiting for them. April held a large ring full of old skeleton keys. She led them through a hallway and down a flight of stairs to the basement. April fumbled with the keys until she found the one etched with a number one. It was the number one key because it was the oldest lock in the building. Immediately after she opened the door the smell of old musty-mildew filled the air. She flipped on the light switch and a long half-lit spooky hallway appeared before them.

"You've got to be kidding me," Claire joked, as she looked at Kate. "We should have brought the boys with us. They would have enjoyed this. April, does anyone ever come down here much?"

"Actually, I was down here a few weeks ago looking for some old building permits. It's not really as bad as it looks. Maintenance tries to get down here once a month to check the mouse traps and maybe change some burnt-out light bulbs. Here we are. This is the archive room. Anything over five years old gets archived down here."

"Look at all this," Kate said, as she stepped into the room and walked along the shelves as she rattled-off titles. "Auto tag registrations, business licenses, real estate property records, marriage records, traffic records, tax records, small claim civil records ... Wait," as she stepped back, "tax records. This is where we should start."

April agreed with Kate that the tax records would be the most logical place to start. So, for the next five nights the girls, including April, searched through more than fifty years of tax records. Then they checked the death records. But they found nothing. Although they did find *one* entry with the name Wendell from 1923, it turned out to be a Mr. Wendell James Parker, who at the time was visiting his daughter and passed away while sleeping. But this couldn't possibly have been their Wendell, because *his* last journal wasn't written until nineteen years *after* 1923.

During those five nights that the girls worked together at the county clerk's office, Kate revealed the story of Wendell to Matilda and April, and the reason they were searching for him. To Kate and Claire's surprise, they didn't laugh. And even though they didn't find any clues about Wendell during their long hours of record searching, Matilda and April were so touched by Kate's story that they asked if they too could be included in their search for Wendell.

Chapter Eight

The research intensified over the next couple weeks, as Josh and Billy recruited several more kids from school to help them read through the journals. Tommy, one of the new recruits whose father owns Hammond's Hardware Store, was glad to help out. This was perfect for the boys; since they were about to ask Mr. Hammond, if he could tell them anything about Wendell's carving tools that they'd found up on the plateau. They figured that since Hammond's was the only hardware store in town, this is where Wendell must have bought his tools. Hammond's Hardware Store was founded by Stub Hammond's father, Albert, way back in the late 1880's, long before Wendell ever came to town.

Mr. Hammond was glad to help the boys in their research. After close examination of one of Wendell's carving tools, he identified it through an older store catalog as being one of many different brands his father carried in the store up through the late 1920's. The next step was to find Wendell's name in one of the old ledgers.

The next day after school, Mr. Hammond took his son Tommy, along with Josh and Billy to the storeroom in the basement where he kept all the store's old ledgers. The boys sat down at a large table situated in the center of the room where all the old ledgers were already sitting in several neat piles.

"Ok, boys," Stub Hammond began, "here is every one of the ledgers from the late 1890's to the late 1920's. Now what you'll want to
be looking at," as he flipped open one of the ledgers, "is the third
column from the left; this will tell the type of tool that was purchased. In this case here, it's a Reynolds 2650D #2C file, and this last
column shows that a Mr. Joseph Coyne paid cash for it. So, just scan
down through the last two columns. What you want to be looking for
is anything that says Stratford. Back then, the only Stratford items
sold in this store were wood carving tools. Today, we carry over fifty
items with the Stratford label. Anyway, look for the Stratford name in
the third column and Wendell's name in the last ... and, good luck
boys."

The first journal Josh picked up was dated way back to 1897,
which according to Wendell's journals, would be his first full year living in Whispering Pines. There were hundreds of entries for the Stratford carving tools, but none were purchased by Wendell. The boys
spent the next few days after school searching through every one of
the ledgers, but the name Wendell never showed up.

The boys and their friends continued reading through Wendell's
journals, while at the same time, began thinking of other ways to try
to locate him. Rusty suggested going to the library and looking
through the old furniture company directories. These not only told
about the company itself, but also gave the names and addresses
of all the employees and what their job functions were. Rusty volunteered to head up that research, down at the library while several
new members of the group: Frank, Joe, Jerry, Dave, Tim and Kristin,
were happy to join him.

During the past few weeks with all Josh and Billy's friends from
school helping, along with their moms Kate and Claire conducting
their own research, the word about the search for Wendell, the lost
elf, had somehow leaked out. Once certain individuals in town
found out about Wendell, especially in a town this size where most

people knew each other, the gossip mill started churning. Soon it was in high gear and there was no stopping it.

Once the local newspaper found out who the ringleader was, a reporter immediately drove to Josh's house to conduct an interview. It was late afternoon, there were ten kids from the boys' research group sitting on the living room floor dividing up journals. They barely began reading, when suddenly, the door bell rang.

Josh jumped up and quickly ran to answer the door, hoping it might be some of the other kids that were invited over to join his and Billy's research group. But when he opened the door he was surprised to see who was standing there.

"Good evening, young man, I'm Roger Thompson from the *Star Gazette*. Is there a Josh Lewis at home?"

"That's me; I'm Josh Lewis. Say, I remember seeing you when my class took a field trip last year to learn how newspapers were made. Why are you looking for me?"

"I'd like to do a story on you and your friend Billy. Is Billy here, too?"

"Yeah ... um ... come on in," Josh said nervously as he led Roger into the kitchen. "I'll be right back, Mr. Thompson. I have to go get Billy."

Josh went back into the living room and told everybody to just keep reading where they left off yesterday while he pulled Billy into the hallway.

"What's the matter with you, Josh?" Billy whispered.

"There's a guy in the kitchen from the *Star Gazette*. He says he wants to do a story on you and me."

"What does he want to do a story on us for?"

"Billy, I don't think it's about us, it's probably about Wendell."

"Oh, so, what do you think we should do, Josh?"

"I'm not sure. If we go and tell him everything we know about Wendell, it's going to be all over town. We'll never hear the end of this at school. They'll make fun of us forever."

"But on the other hand, Josh, maybe someone that knows Wendell will read the story. At least then we'll be able to get those journals back to Wendell. And besides, the kids at school can't make fun of us forever."

"Yeah, maybe you're right, Billy. So, I guess we'll tell Mr. Thompson the story."

The boys walked back into the living room where the other kids were busy reading and talking about the library research they would be doing while Billy picked up the first journal and took it into the kitchen.

The boys spent the first ten minutes telling their story of chasing the rabbit down the ravine and finding the cabin on the plateau. Then they talked about Millie, and how they located the chest full of Wendell's journals hidden within the rock wall. Suddenly, just as Josh began opening Wendell's journal to the first page, Josh's mom Kate walked into the kitchen.

"Hi boys; who's your friend?" Kate said, as she reached across the table to shake Roger's hand.

"He's from the *Star Gazette*, Mom. He wants to do a story about Wendell."

"Actually, Kate, "Roger interjected," I really want to do a story about the boys in their search for Wendell. I thought since the rumors are already floating around town, this would be a good time to put out an official story. Anyway, this town could use a good Christmas article. Maybe it will cast a little bit of that old fashioned Yuletide spirit."

As Kate looked down at Josh and Billy, she began to feel guilty.

"I'm sorry, boys, this is probably my fault. Billy, your mom and I have been trying to help you locate Wendell on our own. We haven't had a lot of luck yet, but we knew this was going to be a big task for both of you and a huge responsibility. We just thought we'd try to help out a little. I suspect the rumors may have started down at the nursing home or maybe at the court house. That's where we did some of our *own* research."

"That's okay, Mom. Billy and I *want* you guys to help us find Wendell. This isn't going to be easy you know. I think writing a story would be a great idea"

Kate looked over at Roger, then back at the boys and smiled. "Okay, I guess it wouldn't hurt anything, would it? Roger, do you think you can write a good enough story to convince your readers that we could use any information they may have to help us locate Wendell?"

"I'll give it my best shot, Kate," Roger said with a smile as he continued writing down more notes for the story.

The next morning, as John opened the front door to get the morning paper, the phone rang. It was Susan Walker from the *Star Gazette*. She was in a semi-panic mode, and needed desperately to speak with Josh. John shrugged his shoulders at his wife as he handed her the phone.

"Hello, this is Josh's mom, Kate Lewis. Can I help you?"

"Yes, thank you. Mrs. Lewis, this is Susan Walker from the *Star Gazette*. I'm sorry to bother you so early in the morning, but for the last hour or so we've been getting non-stop phone calls about that Wendell article. We normally don't get this kind of response from a story, especially this early after the paper's been delivered, so we're a little confused about what we should do."

"What kind of response are you talking about?" Kate asked, in an anxious voice.

"Well, they want to help. They all desperately want to help Josh and Billy find this Wendell person. I guess maybe it's that time of year, you know, when everyone wants to be generous and lend a hand during the holidays."

"Wow, we really didn't expect this kind of response," Kate replied. "As Josh and Billy explained to Roger last night, they've only read through a small portion of the forty-four journals, and if there were any chance at all of finding Wendell by Christmas, we would need to find someone who either knows Wendell or is a relative. But the kind of response you're talking about makes it sound like half the town wants to help."

"That's what it sounds like to us down here, too. We're not sure what to do, Kate, unless you want us to start giving out your number so they can contact you directly!"

"Yes," Kate answered with a gleam of anticipation on her face as she glanced over at John. "That would be just fine with me. It sounds like the boys will be getting more assistance than they expected. Thank you for calling, Susan, and please, feel free to call me back if you need anything else."

As soon as Kate hung up the phone, John gave her a strange look and asked her what she'd agreed to. When she told him, he just hung his head, dropped his shoulders and said, "I have the strangest feeling that you and the boys have just opened up Pandora's Box. What are we going to do if a hundred people call and end up at our front door? We don't have room for all those people. Oh, and by the way, Kate, what are we going to do about Thanksgiving?"

"Don't you worry about that," Kate snapped. "We'll still celebrate Thanksgiving."

John shook his head and then gave her a hug. "Whatever it takes, Kate," he said. "I'm just here to help out. Just let me know what you and the boys need me to do."

Kate immediately got on the phone and called Claire with the news. During the next hour, over twenty people called in response to the article and volunteered their services. Most of them were families with kids, although a few of them were owners of businesses around town, and a few were elderly people just wanting to do what they could.

After Josh was ready for school and walked into the kitchen to eat breakfast, Kate told him about the phone calls she'd been getting. Josh was so excited he threw his school books on the counter and scurried around looking for the newspaper.

"Mom, where's the newspaper?" Josh yelled.

With the phone call from the newspaper first thing this morning and the flood of calls coming in from people wanting to volunteer, John and Kate completely forgot about going outside to get the newspaper. They hadn't even read the article yet. Josh rushed out of the house to get the paper from the front yard. On the way back he fumbled through the pages looking for the article.

"Here it is," Josh yelled, as he entered the kitchen and began to read aloud: Josh and Billy have found a treasure that is quickly becoming the talk of the town. Christmas is alive and well in Whispering Pines, and there are a couple groups of individuals out there who have been spreading the Christmas Spirit. They've been conducting research trying desperately to find some information on the whereabouts of a Christmas elf. His name is Wendell. All they know so far is that Wendell came here to our town on December 24th, 1896. No one really knows what Wendell looks like, but if you have seen anyone in the last fifty six years that even resembles an elf, please call the *Star Gazette*. Let's do our part to help Josh and Billy in their search to find Wendell before Christmas arrives."

"Oh my," Kate whispered. "That explains all the phone calls. Everybody in town is going to want to help." Kate looked at Josh and John as the phone began ringing again.

As Kate hung up the phone she turned and announced that she had an idea.

"Let's have a meeting, you know, a kickoff to get others from around town involved to help your group," as she looked at Josh. "They can help us read through all those journals. Some of the elderly may have known or worked with Wendell at one of the old factories in town. We already know he worked at one of them." Josh and John agreed, and decided that tonight at six o'clock they would hold their first meeting. "Okay," Kate commanded, "Josh, you spread the word to your friends at school and have their parents come as well. John, invite some people from your work, and I'll call Claire back and we'll spread the word around the nursing home."

Chapter Nine

*J*ust before six that evening Josh and Billy stood, looking out the living room window as a swarm of cars began filling up both sides of the street.

"Here they come, Mom," Josh yelled, as Kate rushed over to the window to take a peek.

"Oh my goodness," Kate said, as she grabbed Claire by the arm. "Where on earth are we going to put all these people? We don't have that many chairs."

Kate yelled for John and Bob to come into the living room to do some quick rearranging of the furniture. Billy and Josh went out to the back porch and grabbed the folding chairs, then, they picked up the kitchen and dining room chairs, and did a quick run through the house to gather anything else that could be used to sit on. But, within the next ten minutes, the living room was standing room only.

"Josh," Kate whispered, as she pulled him toward her. "I'm going to go up front and say a few words to these people and then I want you and Billy to come up and tell everyone how you found the journals and about some of the research you've been doing. If you want all these people to help us find Wendell, then this is the time to ask them. Hey, you convinced me and your dad. And Billy, you convinced your parents, so don't worry, I'm sure you'll be able to convince everyone here."

Kate started the meeting off by thanking everyone for coming and then gave a quick overview about what she and Claire have been working on and what they planned to do for the next few days. She also made it clear that most of what they needed right now was information. "We have to get out and talk to people, specifically the elderly," Kate stressed. "These are the people who might have worked with or may have been acquaintances of Wendell's."

Josh and Billy immediately captured everyone's attention with several quick stories from Wendell's journals. They also explained how they stumbled upon the chest. But most of all, they guided the people through their process of reading through enough of the journal to make sense of it, then to go out and begin researching to find some answers. Josh gave them several examples of where Wendell had mentioned people and places by name to use as stepping stones to begin their research.

After Josh and Billy were finished, Kate asked everyone in the room to divide into groups of five. Starting with the sixth journal, each group was given one journal to read through and search for any clues that might lead them to a person, store, church, organization, or anything that could be a possible lead.

Josh and Billy, along with their moms and dads, were all standing together watching the individual groups thumbing through the journals while others were kicking around ideas of their own.

"I think it's going pretty well," Kate said.

"Yeah, Mom, if all these groups can read through all the journals and take some good notes, we're bound to have enough information to find Wendell."

"Excuse me, "Kate yelled. "Now that each group has had a chance to read through some of their journal and talk about a few ideas, there's just one more thing I'd like to add. These journals must remain in this house. We cannot take the risk of even one of these journals getting lost. We can meet here every evening from six to eight. That will give everyone enough time to get home and eat dinner first. Also, I'd like to thank you all for coming here tonight and taking a personal interest in helping us find Wendell, and we hope to see you all back here tomorrow."

Since most of the journals hadn't even been touched yet, the search to find Wendell had *really* just begun. For the next few days, before Thanksgiving, then immediately after, the journal reading and research continued. Soon, word about the forty-four journals and the search for Wendell began spreading to more and more people throughout town.

Several groups began to build a timeline surrounding all the events Wendell had recorded in his journals; where he went every day, the stores he patronized, the church he attended, any parks he visited, where he worked, ate, and so forth. As a result, a picture began to emerge about how he lived his life and the people he might have encountered. Throughout the last week in November, the group was able to read and document about seventy five percent of the journals. At that point, they combined all the smaller groups into two large groups. One group, headed up by Josh and Billy, was assigned to journal research, while the other group, led by Kate and Claire, was charged with pavement-pounding. The latter set off on their quest to find answers from what had already been documented by the journal research group.

First and foremost came the critical task of locating the person that Wendell called Rush. This would be no easy task. Not only was the information nearly fifty-six years old, but few furniture factories were still in operation. Over the years, the furniture-making business had become more competitive, with only the strongest companies surviving. The bigger factories either swallowed up the smaller ones, or they just simply drove them out of business. As a result, tracking down the owners and employees of those businesses would be extremely difficult.

But before they started their interviewing process around town, with the few leads they already had from Wendell's journals, they decided to make a stop at the library.

When the small army of "pavement-pounders" walked into the library, they followed Kate and Claire to the archive room, which was located through a narrow doorway on the left side of the back wall. The room was massive with ceiling-high bookshelves made of dark maple that surrounded the room. Two ladders, attached to the shelves by upper and lower tracks, were located at each side of the room for retrieving those hard to reach books on the upper shelves. The girls quickly divided the group into pairs before they were seated. Four large rectangular tables, lined up perpendicular to each other, stretched across the room. Hanging from the ceiling were three large bowl-shaped lights on long chains, while numerous brass lights with dark green glass covers adorned the tabletops. Kate and Claire quickly scoured the shelves and began pulling down some of the old factory books and started passing them out. The sound of pages turning and people chatting quickly filled the air.

In no time at all the chatter turned to shouts as family members' names and older friends and acquaintances began appearing on the pages. Suddenly, the head librarian stepped in the room and asked the group to quiet down. Everyone looked at each other and suddenly broke out laughing.

After about two hours of sifting through countless old factory archives in search of familiar names, the group finally had a list of people they could talk to. Kate and Claire walked around the room to scan everyone's list to see if they could recognize any names from the nursing home.

"Wiley Perkins," Kate said aloud. "He's one of my patients. You can scratch *him* off your list, Gary. I'll talk to Mr. Perkins first thing in the morning."

Claire recognized three of her patients names on other lists and couldn't wait to get to work in the morning to talk to them. The group left the library and headed home. The next day after work they would begin interviewing people from their list.

When Kate arrived at the nursing home the next morning, she grabbed a quick cup of coffee and immediately walked down the hall to Mr. Perkins room. Kate knew that he'd already be up reading the morning paper. He made it a morning ritual to keep current with the happenings around town and the rest of the world. He was also a big history buff and read tons of books on a variety of subjects ranging from the fall of the Roman Empire to the Civil War.

"Good morning, Mr. Perkins," Kate announced, as she slowly strolled into the room, taking care not to startle him.

His eyes always lit up when he saw her, and he quickly folded his newspaper up and placed it on his lap.

"Well, hi there Kate. What brings you into work so early this morning?"

"Actually, I'm working on a big project at home and I'd like to ask you some questions. That is, if you don't mind."

"Let me guess," Mr. Perkins spouted off. "Does it have anything to do with that newspaper article about Josh and Billy?"

"As a matter of fact, it does," Kate answered.

"Then go right ahead, Kate. I'm not sure if I can help you, but you have my undivided attention."

"Well, it's a long story, and there isn't a lot of time to go into details. As you already know, from what was in the newspaper, my son Josh and his friend Billy recently found an old chest up in the woods at the site of an old collapsed cabin. The chest was packed full of journals dating all the way back to 1896. Now, as far as we can tell, they belonged to a person by the name of Wendell. Now this is where I need your help. Do you know of a Wendell or did you work with somebody by that name when you worked at the furniture factory?"

"Wendell? Let me think for a second. No, can't recall ever know-ing anyone by that name, and I may be old, Kate, but I have a good memory when it comes to names."

"What about the name Rush; does that one ring a bell?"

"Rush ... Rush," Mr. Perkins repeated, looking up at Kate with a gleam in his eyes. "Now that's a name I haven't heard in quite a long time! My old buddy Rush ..."

"So you know him? You know who Rush is?"

"Sure, I knew Rush, but he's been gone for a long time now, passed away the same year that the Titanic hit that iceberg and sank in the ocean. But Rush was just his nickname. His real name was Paul Strait, and he was a very close friend of mine. Back then every-one in town knew who Rush was. He owned the Strait Manufactur-ing Company and made some of the finest furniture around. The factory's all gone now. They ended up tearing it down several years back to put up that big plaza. You know, it's the one with that Wool-worth's five and dime store."

"Did you work for Rush?" Kate questioned, sounding like a private investigator.

"No, I worked for another firm called the Lambert Manufacturing Company. Rush and I, well ... we grew up together."

Kate continued asking more questions about some of the things Wendell mentioned in the journals, to see if anything sounded famil-iar to him. After about thirty minutes Mr. Perkins couldn't think of any-thing else to say, so Kate thanked him for his time and left the room.

As she started walking down the hallway, Mr. Perkins called out for her to come back. She immediately ran back to his room thinking something was wrong.

"Sam!" he shouted, as Kate stood in the doorway. "His name was Sam, Kate. He was a small man. He couldn't have been more than four and a half feet tall. And he had a thin white beard. I remember when Rush first hired him. He told me that Sam came to his office one day looking for work, Rush said he just showed up out of the blue. So Rush gave him a block of wood along with some carving tools and asked him to carve him something, *anything*. That was the job interview. That's the way Rush conducted his business. That squirrel, the one you mentioned from the journals, that is what Sam carved for Rush. It didn't hit me until you walked out of the room. We used to call him "Silent Sam" because he was so quiet. To this day, I have never seen anyone that could carve anything with such perfection. It was beautiful. He was quite the craftsman. Rush used to tell me stories about all the things he would carve during his spare time."

"Do you know what ever happened to Sam?" Kate asked.

"Well … after Rush passed away, his son took charge of the company and continued running it until they were forced to shut down. I would still visit Rush's son now and then over at the factory and Sam was still there, always keeping busy. I never heard a word about where Sam disappeared to though. But I can tell you that Rush's factory shut down in 1940. I remember that year very clearly because that's the same year I lost my job."

Kate was so excited that she bent over the bed and gave Mr. Perkins a kiss on the cheek.

Later that evening, Kate filled everyone in on the talk she had with Mr. Perkins and what she had learned about Rush. Then, soon after Kate had finished, eight members of her and Claire's pavement-pounding group had good news of their own. Even though they had all talked to different people, they all had similar stories. Back in the early 1900's, everyone in this small town of Whispering Pines seemed to know each other. They had story after story about Rush, but very few had any recollections of Sam.

Well, one thing was for sure. Now they knew Wendell had an alias: Sam.

"Why didn't Wendell use his real name?" Billy asked out loud.

"Maybe he didn't want anyone to know who he really was," someone replied.

Suddenly everyone in the room started spouting off negative theories. Maybe he was hiding from the law because he'd robbed a bank or something. Yeah, maybe he was just laying low for a while.

"Maybe he murdered someone, or ..."

"Or, maybe he really *was* an elf, just as the journals say. Maybe he just didn't want anyone to know about it," Tom Dunkel announced. He then looked back down at the journal he was reading while everyone turned around and stared back at him. "He says it all right here in this journal I'm reading. He talks about everything in here, and it's just so realistic. This is the last journal he wrote, in 1940. He writes in detail about the gold chain that Josh told us about, and how he lost it falling out of Santa's sleigh. He even tells about how Fulton, an elfin friend I presume, used to clean and repair his watch, and how much he misses everyone. He hints about making toys on several occasions, but he mostly talks about searching for his chain so he can get back home."

"That's right," Josh declared. "The gold chain has to be attached to his watch for some reason. At least, that's what it said in the first journal, but we never read anywhere in the journals whether or not he'd found it."

"Well," Tom said, thumbing through the last few pages of the last journal, "he doesn't seem to have found it in this last journal *either*."

Several people in the room suggested that the chain must have been something he made up. Maybe even the whole story was fabricated. The person who wrote these journals, whether he'd been Wendell or Sam, was probably long gone by now anyway. The search for Wendell seemed to die right then and there. It turned out that Wendell was really Silent Sam and he was nowhere to be found. There was never any mention of family, and after reading through that last journal, Wendell sounded more and more like a crazy man rather than the typical fictional elf character you read about.

Chapter Ten

$\mathcal{A}$fter everyone left the house that night, a very depressed Josh and Billy gathered up all the journals and took them upstairs to Josh's room. As they were placing them back on the shelf, Billy told Josh that he still believed in Wendell and that they should keep on searching. Josh's eyes suddenly lit up. He was convinced that after what everyone had to say at the meeting Billy wouldn't want to help anymore either.

Within the next few days the rumors and excitement about Wendell and his journals seemed to have faded away. But not for Kate and Claire, they actually shared the boys' belief and were secretly reading through the journals every chance they had. Even though they were all greatly disappointed that the whole town suddenly stopped believing in Wendell, they were determined to find some answers.

About eight thirty the next morning, a somewhat depressed Kate shuffled into work. She was then informed that one of the second floor nurses called in sick and she would also have to cover her rounds for the day as well. She knocked and pushed open the door to her first patient, then reached around and lifted the clipboard off the hook hanging on the back of the door. While she scanned through the patient's vital signs from the night shift, she noticed the name at the top of the sheet. Sam. But there was no last name. A big smile formed across Kate's face as she bowed her head and slowly moved it from side to side as she thought about Wendell.

"Good old Sam," she whispered to herself.

Per the information on the chart, this Sam not only didn't have a last name, there was also no next of kin. As Kate turned around, she was instantly drawn to all the shelves adorning the walls. The shelves were packed full with a variety of wooden figures and characters. It was amazing.

"Good morning," Sam said, as he broke Kate's train-of-thought. "Where's Betty. Is she out sick today?"

"Um … yes, she called in with a bad headache and said she wouldn't be able to make it in today."

Kate slowly walked to the side of the bed. "Good morning, my name is Kate, and I'll be taking over Betty's duties today," as she tried to compose herself. "And how are you feeling this morning, Sam?"

"Very old, Kate … thanks for asking though. How are *you* doing, you seem a little preoccupied? Is there something on your mind that you don't mind sharing with an old man?"

"No, no, I'm fine Sam. It's probably all this holiday hustle and bustle, that's all. Christmas is just around the corner you know. That in itself is enough to keep the mind running in circles."

Sam was right. She was preoccupied. This whole Wendell thing had her head spinning. She tried three times to take Sam's pulse before she finally got it right. After she finished, she gazed back around the room at all the carvings again, then slowly walked back towards the door and hung up the clipboard. As she opened the door and stepped out into the hallway, she turned around and said, "See you in a few hours, Wendell," and shut the door. She took about three steps down the hallway before she realized what she had done. She immediately stopped in her tracks. "I just called him Wendell," she whispered to herself.

She turned around and immediately walked back to his room, slowly opened the door, and stuck her head inside.

"Sorry Sam. I didn't mean to call you that. It's just a name of one of the characters in a book I've been reading. I wasn't thinking ..."

"How did you know?" Sam asked, as he slowly sat up in his bed. "How did you know that my real name was Wendell?"

Kate froze in the doorway. She was speechless.

"You ... you're ... Wendell?" she asked, slowly closing the door behind her.

"Yes, I am Wendell. I take it you must have found my journals."

"My son Josh and his friend Billy found them about two months ago."

"How could you have known it was me from reading those journals? I don't remember ever writing the name Sam in there."

"We've been doing a lot of research lately and found out that Rush had once hired a person by the name of Sam. It turns out that Sam carved him a squirrel. After the boys found the squirrel and we read it in one of your journals, we just put two and two together. But I never dreamed you were *that* Sam. I called you Wendell by accident. When I saw your name was Sam on the clipboard, I instantly thought of Wendell."

"But you were right," Sam replied, "I am Wendell. Well ... I was Wendell, a long time ago."

"What do you mean? You still are Wendell, and why have you been calling yourself Sam all these years?"

"Because, Wendell is my elfin name; you see, Kate, after I lost my chain in the fall I was no longer an elf. The magic was gone. That's why I've grown so old, and soon ... I shall die."

Kate wanted desperately to stay and talk more with Sam, but she knew she had to locate Claire and then they had to go pull the boys out of school to tell them the news. She asked if it'd be okay to bring the boys and Claire back later to sit down and talk. He said yes and gave her a big smile as she left the room. He was relieved that his secret was finally out in the open.

Chapter Eleven

*W*ithin the hour, Kate and Claire found a couple nurses to take over their duties for the day and rushed-off to get the boys out of school. Thirty minutes later, they were back at the nursing home. As they arrived on the second floor, the boys began jumping with joy as they walked down the hallway toward Wendell's room. Wendell did this, Wendell did that, they said, jabbering about every little detail they'd read about in the journals. Claire was still shocked at what Kate had told her. She just couldn't believe that the Wendell they'd all been searching for was right here in their very own nursing home.

Kate slowly pushed the door open and stuck her head inside to see if Sam was awake.

"We're here Sam. Is it okay if we come in now?" Kate whispered.

"Well, hello again, Kate; Yes, come on in, everybody, I've been waiting for you."

"Hello, Sam," Kate said. "This is my friend Claire. She's also a nurse here at the nursing home and works on the first floor with me. And this is my son, Josh and Claire's son, Billy. These are the boys who found your chest full of journals, Sam."

"Well, it's nice to meet all of you. So, now that you've found my journals and already read through some of them, you must have a lot of questions for me?"

"Just a couple Wendell ... I mean Sam."

"Sure Josh, go right ahead."

"Are you really the Christmas elf from the North Pole that you said you were in the journals?"

"Yes I am," Sam answered. "At least, I was until I lost my gold chain."

"That was my second question, Sam. So there really is a gold chain, and a watch and all that other stuff that you wrote about in the journals; it's all true?"

"Josh, elves can't tell a lie. And even though I haven't considered myself an elf since I lost my gold chain, I will still, always, tell the truth. So to answer your question, yes, everything I wrote in those journals is definitely the truth."

"I can honestly tell you all that I really was an elf, and my name was Wendell. I was one of Santa's elves for more than 100 years. The only reason I was even with Santa that night was because of the lottery. Every year Santa had that lottery to see what lucky elf would get to go along and help Santa deliver the presents. That was the first time I'd ever won. While we were making our last deliveries that night, I got a little careless as I climbed over the seat to grab a present for the next delivery. That's when I slipped and fell out. It was my own fault. Santa always said to wait until the sleigh came to a full stop before I pulled the next present out of the bag. But towards the end of our deliveries that night, I thought I'd surprise Santa by giving him the next present before he asked for it. That's when it happened. That's how I lost my life-chain."

Everyone in the room was speechless.

"Listen, everyone. I know this is difficult for you to accept," Sam pleaded, trying desperately to convince them. "Please, Josh, go over to the center drawer of the bureau and bring me the small wooden box."

When Josh opened the drawer, he saw the wooden box and instantly recognized the **W** carved into the top.

"Yup, this is Wendell's all right," as Josh turned around to display the **W** to everyone. He carved this letter **W** into everything."

"Thank you," Sam said, as Josh handed him the wooden box. "I think once you've all seen what I have in here you'll be convinced that I am who I say I am."

Sam slowly opened the lid of the box, reached inside, and pulled out a gold pocket watch. Everyone moved closer as he held it up for all to see. It's like no watch they had ever seen before. It was slightly smaller than a normal pocket watch, with a casing of bright gold, and a cone shaped diamond winder located at the top that sparkled with all the colors of the rainbow.

"Here at the top center of the diamond is the threaded hole where my chain was once attached. The watch hasn't ticked now for all of fifty-six years. Never could find that gold chain. Looked everywhere for it. Finally had to give up the search; I just got too old."

"What's in that little pouch?" Billy asked, as he pointed to the corner of the opened box.

"That, my new friends, is what's going to convince you that I'm telling the truth. I've never really had a use for this stuff until now."

Sam pulled out the soft leather pouch from the box, placed it on his lap and carefully loosened the strings.

"This here is the last of my magical dust," Sam announced. "I hope there's enough, though, to make you believe. I'm going to show you what I looked like when I was Wendell, but keep in mind, this is only going to be temporary, and it will only last a few seconds, so don't blink."

As everyone in the room held their breath, Sam lifted the bag up over his head. They all knew that something incredible was about to happen.

"Please, don't be afraid by what you're about to see. Remember, this is only temporary," Sam said, as he poured the entire bag of magic dust over his head.

Everyone watched the magic dust as it slowly fell out of the bag and filled the air above Sam's head. Several minutes seemed to pass before the dust actually touched his hair, but then his whole appearance started to change right before their eyes. His thin off-white hair instantly turned a thick snowy white while his pointed ears poked up through. As the dust fell across his face, the wrinkles quickly disappeared, leaving a tighter flesh-colored skin, and then a long white flowing beard started to appear. Finally, a forest green stocking cap with a red furry brim and matching ball at the end quickly formed around his head.

Wendell gave a quick smile and a wink, and then in an instant, he turned back into Sam. The whole episode lasted only seconds, but it was more than enough time to convince everyone in the room.

"You really *are* an elf," said a shocked and bewildered Josh, as he and Billy began jumping and yelling around the room.

"Then the stories really are true," Kate interjected. "You were Wendell … and you really were an elf."

Sam carefully placed the empty pouch and his gold pocket watch back into the box and gently closed the lid.

"Here," he said, lifting the box up to Josh, "I want you to keep this in a safe place for me; keep it with the journals. My time is coming to an end soon, and you four are the only ones who know who I truly am. Please, this is very important to me. When they put me to rest, this box, along with its contents, must remain with me. The magic of Christmas must stay in the imagination of everyone, and these items must not be exploited. Please promise me that you'll do this one thing for me when the time comes."

The boys, along with Kate and Claire, gave Sam their word and assured him that the box would remain safe and hidden until that time came. Then they said their goodbyes for the night and left the room.

Around eleven o'clock that evening, Claire suddenly opened her eyes and sat up in bed. "We forgot to ask him about the gold chain," she whispered, throwing her legs over the bed and stepping into her bedroom slippers. She crept slowly out of the bedroom and walked downstairs to the kitchen to call Kate. She wasn't concerned about the time. This was too important to wait until tomorrow.

"Kate," Claire whispered, "I'm sorry to call you so late, but there's something we forgot to ask Sam. The chain ... we didn't question him about how he really lost his gold chain."

"Claire, what are you talking about? He explains all that in the journals."

"That can't be all there is Kate, there has to be more to it than what he wrote in those journals. Sam *has* to be able to remember more than that. Something has got to be missing."

"I think you may be right, Claire, he also didn't ask us to go back up to the plateau to look for it either."

"All Sam really talked about was dying," Kate said.

"Maybe just because *he* failed to find it, he didn't think anyone else would be able to either. He's just lost hope, Kate. Sam gave up a long time ago."

"You're right, Claire, he hasn't told us the whole story. Maybe what he wrote in the journals was only part of what actually happened. We'll talk to him first thing in the morning."

Chapter Twelve

*E*arly the next morning, Kate and Claire walked into the front door of the nursing home two hours before their shift started and went directly to Sam's room. As Kate eased the door open a crack, she could see Sam sitting up in his bed holding one of his wooden carvings.

"Is it okay if we come in for a visit, Sam?" Kate asked in a whisper.

"Sure it is! Good morning, ladies. Of course you can come in. I was just doing a little reminiscing. Grab yourselves a chair and sit down. You two are here awfully early this morning. What's on your minds?"

"Sam," Claire said, glancing over at Kate, "we'd like to know more about your gold chain you lost. The boys and their friends have been reading through your journals, but we'd like to hear the whole story from you, including all the details. It might help us out when we start searching for it."

"My gold chain," Sam repeated, looking back down at the carving in his hands, which he had carved long ago. "See this carving? It's one of the first ones I did after Rush hired me to work at his furniture factory. It's a carving of my best friend Fulton. He's the master watchmaker up at the North Pole. He did all the repairs and cleaning, too. Every year he would come to my workbench to clean and shine my pocket watch for me, right there on the spot. He did that for everyone though, that was his job, but he always spent a little more time on mine. We were really good friends, Fulton and I. I really do miss him."

"That's what we wanted to talk to you about, Sam," Kate said. "If you could find that chain, would you become Wendell again? You know, like yesterday, but permanently?"

Sam looked up at Kate and cocked his head to one side the way a dog does when it can't quite comprehend what you're saying.

"Yes ... yes I would," Sam replied. "That chain was my lifeline. It will most definitely, give me back my youth. I would be able to ..." Sam stopped talking and leaned his head back against the pillow. "It's no use, though girls. I've already looked. I searched that area up there year after year, and I never even found a trace of it. It's gone, and soon, I will be, too."

"Where do you think it is, Sam?" Kate asked emotionally, "We want to help you find it. If we can get enough people searching around that giant pine up by your old cabin, we should have a good chance of finding it. We'll get the whole town involved if that's what it'll take. Sam, you're going to have to help us first, if you want us to help you."

"Sam," Claire chimed in, "didn't you ever ask anyone to help you before? You must have had some friends you could have shared your story with. I'm sure they would have helped."

"I had a few friends at work and around town, but I just didn't want to bother anyone. It didn't feel right for me, a stranger in town, asking someone else for help. I didn't know how to explain it to them. I couldn't compose the proper words to make them believe in me. They would have laughed at me and ran me out of town. There was only one person in this whole town who I confided in, and she never once asked how I lost that gold chain. Her name was Millie. She used to live in the house at the foot of the plateau."

"She still does, Sam. She's the one who told our boys about your gold chain."

"Millie, the boys talked to my Millie. How is she, is she doing well? When was the last time they spoke to her?"

"Actually, Kate and I talked to her less than a month ago; around the same time I found your chest sitting behind my garage. Long story ... don't ask. Anyway, we read her name in your journal and we drove down there to talk to her, taking a chance that she might be the same person. We asked her if she knew anyone by the name of Wendell and where we could find him. She didn't tell us much, only that she couldn't wait to see the look on your face when you found that gold chain."

"Millie," Sam whispered, after sitting silent for a moment. "We used to be the best of friends. We would take long walks in the woods together, and sometimes we'd end up staying gone for the better part of the day. Other times we would sit and just talk into the wee hours of the night while I did some wood carving on the front porch. The day I left to move in here, she probably thought I was just going to work. I never told her I was leaving. I never said goodbye. I couldn't ... I just couldn't say goodbye to her."

Sam went on to explain in detail what happened the night he fell from the sky.

"When I woke up the next morning, I was laying flat on my back in about a foot of snow. At first I thought I was paralyzed. But then, after a few minutes, the feeling started to come back into my legs and arms, and I was able to roll over onto my side. When I reached in my pocket and pulled out my watch, I noticed immediately that the crystal had a hairline crack in it. Then I noticed that the gold chain was gone. The watch hands had stopped moving at one minute before midnight. Time always stands still on Christmas Eve. It stands still for Santa. That's how he's able to deliver his presents all over the world. That's the time I fell from the sleigh and onto the giant pine tree. My chain was gone, my watch had stopped, and the aging process had begun.

"I rolled over onto my back again and gazed around. Everything was strange to me. The first thing I noticed was the giant pine tree I fell out of, and then as I looked further, I spotted a small cabin. The whole area was surrounded mostly in pine trees, some birch trees, and a mixture of oak and cedar. After a few minutes, I got up and made my way over to the cabin where I found the door unlocked. When I walked inside, I discovered the place was empty, except for a small bed in the corner. At the foot of the bed there was a neatly folded blanket with a pillow on top. Everything in the room was neat and organized, but heavily covered in a thick layer of dust. I figured it would be safe to say that no one would be showing up anytime soon, so I crawled onto the bed, covered over with the blanket and fell asleep.

"When I woke up again, it was pitch-black out. As I sat up in the bed, I could hear the wind howling. I tried to push the front door open, but it was jammed. Then as I looked out the front window there was a solid wall of snow. That's when I realized there had been a snowstorm and the snow had probably drifted up against the front door. I crawled back under the covers and fell into a deep sleep until morning.

"During the next couple of days, I made my way down from the plateau and met Millie and her parents. They invited me into their house, fed me, and treated me like part of their family. They even gave me permission to stay in the cabin for as long as I liked. The very next day Millie took me into town and showed me around. That's when I first met Rush. He hired me to work for him that very same day. Millie sat there while I carved that squirrel for him."

"Now that I had a place to live and a good job to buy the things I needed, I began my search for the chain. Every bit of spare time I had I searched for it. Sometimes Millie would come up to the cabin and help in the search, but most of the time it was just me. My nights were spent carving portraits of all my friends at the North Pole, since that was a good way to keep their faces fresh in my mind, and writing in my journal. As the years went by with no sign of the chain, I figured it must have got hung up on the sleigh when I fell out. That was the summer of 1940 … the last time I searched for the gold chain, the last year I wrote in the journals, and the last time I saw Millie. That's when I moved in here. Until you two and the boys showed up here yesterday, I had lost all hope. But now you've given me new hope, something to look forward to."

"I'm so sorry, Sam," Kate said, as she held his hand. "Are you sure you looked everywhere for that chain? There are a lot of trees and rocks up there. The boys said there was a big ravine up there, did you check there? What about the creek? It could have been anywhere up there."

"I only checked about a 200 foot radius around the tree I fell from. That was the only logical place that made sense for me to look."

Two hours had gone by, and it was time for the girls to start work. They said their goodbyes to Sam and left the room.

"It must have gotten caught up in that tree," Kate said, as she and Claire walked to the nurses' locker room.

"What makes you think that, Kate?"

"Just a hunch, that's the only thing that makes any sense. Plus, that's the only place he didn't mention."

"So, what are we supposed to do now?" Claire asked, as they left the locker room.

"First, we're going to tell the boys everything Sam told us. Then we'll call, beg, and plead with the volunteers to come back for one more meeting. Those people need to be told what happened at the nursing home yesterday. We have to convince them that Sam *is* really Wendell. An even greater challenge is that they have to *believe* us. Then we have to start searching for that gold chain, Claire, before it's too late."

Chapter Thirteen

*D*uring and after work that day, Kate and Claire began making
phone calls trying to convince all the members in the group to
come back for one last meeting. After some serious pleading,
everyone finally gave in and agreed to come back to Kate's house
that night to hear the latest news. At seven o'clock that evening,
people started arriving. By seven fifteen, Kate, with Josh at her side,
walked to the front of the room and asked everyone to listen very
carefully to what she had to say.

At first, everyone seemed a bit standoffish, but when Kate told
everyone that Sam, who was really Wendell, was right under their
noses the whole time, they all perked up. The excitement seemed
to be coming back and they all cheered. Kate spoke for a few
more minutes about their talk with Sam, and then she turned it over
to Josh. Unfortunately, Josh came on a tad bit too strong with the
start of his story. It would have been smoother if he had told them
about all the carved animals and figures that were displayed
around the room, or the watch that was kept in the box. But he
didn't. He went right to the part that was the biggest shock of all,
the part that Billy, Kate, Claire and himself would carry with them for
the rest of their lives; The magic dust. As soon as Josh starting talking
about the magic dust, people began heading for the door, at
which point Billy quickly ran over and blocked their way.

"Wait a second, everyone!" Claire shouted, as she begged everyone to come back into the room. "Josh is telling you the truth. Kate and I were there, too. You have to believe us."

"Listen to me everybody, please," Kate pleaded. "The Sam that's lying in a bed down at the nursing home is the Wendell we've all been searching for. Everything he told us that was written in those journals is true. He explained some of it in such vivid detail that it felt like *we* were actually there. That's when he used the magic dust and changed into Wendell right before our eyes, just to prove to us that he was truly Wendell. Why would we stand up here and tell you all of this if it wasn't true? What would be the point of that, face it people ... elves are real, and *Wendell* is the real thing. He didn't ask for our help. He's just lying in bed waiting to die. He had lost all hope of ever finding that gold chain twelve years ago, but with your help, maybe there's still a chance. Come on everyone, what do you say, where's your Christmas spirit?"

The room fell silent for a moment. Then people started to whisper, and then the excitement began to fill them once again.

"Okay," shouted Jimmy Smith, as he stood up facing Josh and Billy, "I'm in boys, and so are my wife and son. Just tell us where to start looking."

"You can put *me* down on that list too boys," said Mrs. Jenkins from the library. "I can't do any searching around in those hills, but I'll be able to help feed the troops and do whatever else I can from down here on the home front."

Suddenly, the room was once again filled with enthusiastic volunteers. The boys and their moms were ecstatic. They all decided to start searching around the giant pine tree again, right where Sam had left off. Frank Pierce, Grady Brooks, and Keith Logan were ex-lumberjacks and volunteered to climb up and search every crevice of the giant tree. Everyone agreed to meet at the base of the plateau the next day at four o'clock in the afternoon. Billy and Josh weren't exactly sure what tree Wendell was talking about in his journals because there were so many big trees close to the cabin, but all the same, they couldn't wait to show everyone what they had discovered. The news about Wendell refueled the boys' desire to continue the search as well.

By nine o'clock, the meeting was over and everyone left. The boys, along with their moms and dads, sat in the living room and began planning their strategy to search for Wendell's gold chain. They knew the main focus would be on the giant pine tree, but the surrounding area also had to be searched. As soon as Bob started talking about some of the equipment they would need, the phone rang and John quickly jumped up to answer it.

"Hello," John said.

"Hello, Mr. Lewis, this is Rhonda Chambers from the nursing home. May I please speak to Kate? It's very important."

"It's Rhonda, from the nursing home," John said, as he slowly handed the phone to Kate.

The girls made quick eye contact as Kate reached for the phone. The only time anyone from the nursing home ever called them at home was if there was an emergency.

"Hello?" Kate said.

"Hi Kate, this is Rhonda. I'm sorry to bother you at home, but they just rushed Sam to the hospital. Kate … he's had a stroke. It all happened so fast. I was taking his vital signs, and he was telling me about how much he enjoyed visiting with you, Claire, and the boys this morning and then in an instant, the whole right side of his face went limp. It's affected the whole right side of his body, Kate."

"Oh my God," Kate whispered into the phone, as she tried fighting back her tears. "Thanks for calling, Rhonda. I'm going over to the hospital right now. I'll give you a call later."

As soon as Kate hung up the phone, she began to weep. Everyone knew it had to be about Sam.

"Sam's had a stroke. They've taken him over to St. Joseph's. Rhonda said it was his whole right side. What are we going to do now?"

"We need to go see him, Mom!" Josh said. "We're the only family he has. We have to go see him."

On the way to the hospital, Kate informed everyone in the car that the search would still be on for tomorrow, just as they planned.

"Sam's stroke can't put the search on hold. He told us that when his chain is reconnected to his watch, it acts just like the magic dust did. Isn't that right, Claire? Isn't that what Sam told us yesterday after he turned into Wendell?"

"Yes, Kate, but he's had a stroke now. Won't that change things?"

"Why should it? He's still alive. It shouldn't matter," Kate said, as she began raising her voice.

Not another word was spoken the rest of the way to the hospital.

When they arrived, Kate and Claire, with the boys trailing close behind, ran straight back to the intensive care unit. Kate already knew Doctor Gaylord was on the schedule to work nights this week. It was standard procedure for the nursing home to keep a weekly schedule of the hospital staff on call just in case there was an emergency. As Kate pushed open the door, Doctor Mike Gaylord was taking Sam's pulse.

"How is he, Mike?" Kate inquired, in a somber tone.

Kate and the doctor had been friends for years and had always been on a first name basis.

"He's had a bad stroke, Kate. Is he one of your patients?"

"Yes he is. Sam's a good man, Mike, and he has a good heart."

"He has a *strong* heart, I can tell you that," Mike elaborated. "He seems to be quite a fighter, Kate. Normally someone his age wouldn't have been able to survive a stroke this severe, but still, the next forty-eight hours will be crucial for him. I've done all I can do at this point. Now we just have to wait and see."

"He's a very special person, Mike. He'll make it. He *has* to," Kate insisted.

After Doctor Gaylord left the room, Josh and Billy slowly walked over and stood by Sam's bed-side. Sam looked up at them and smiled as best he could. The boys told Sam all about their plans to go back up to the plateau to search for his gold chain. While Josh and Billy began rattling off the names of all the kids and adults that had volunteered to help search for the chain, Kate walked over and pulled them away so that Sam could get some rest.

"Sam," Kate whispered, "we're going to let you get some rest now. We'll be back to see you in the morning." He looked up, smiled and slowly lifted his left hand and waved.

Later that night, Josh couldn't stop thinking about Sam as he lay awake in bed. He worried that the phone was going to ring, at any minute, and someone at the other end was going to tell his mom that Sam had died in his sleep. He kept trying to reassure himself that that was not going to happen ..."he has to live," Josh whispered. Sam was going be fine, and he and Billy, with the help of their parents, and all their friends from all over town, were going to find that gold chain.

Chapter Fourteen

*T*he next morning, while Josh sat at the kitchen table eating a bowl of cereal and Kate was working on her second cup of coffee, they began writing a list of things they needed for their trip to the plateau.

"Good morning, guys. How long have you two been up?" John asked as he reached for the coffee pot and poured himself a cup of coffee.

"About an hour," Kate answered, "Since I couldn't stop thinking about Sam, and Josh was up reading one of Wendell's journals, we decided to come down here to start a list of things we'll need to bring tonight after we get off of work. I don't want us to get all the way up to the plateau and then have to turn around and come back just because we forgot something. It's always best to make a list."

Kate left for work an hour early to stop by the hospital to see how Sam was doing. When she arrived at the intensive care unit, Mike was just leaving Sam's room.

"Good morning, Kate," Mike said.

"Hi, Mike. How's Sam doing this morning? Did he wake up yet? How are his vital signs? I've been checking ..."

"Slow down Kate. Take a breather and calm down a bit. Sam's doing just fine. As a matter of fact, he's doing better than fine. While

I was checking his pulse this morning, he pulled his arm away. I guess it was his way of trying to get my attention to tell me something. So I bent down to let him whisper in my ear."

"What did he say?" Kate asked, as her eyes lit up. "What did he tell you, Mike?"

"It was difficult to hear him at first, but after he repeated it a second time, he said he wanted to know when he could go back to the nursing home. He said hospitals were only for sick people."

Kate was ecstatic. Sam was going to be okay. She couldn't wait to tell Claire and the boys. Now she could go to work without having to worry so much. After work, Kate stopped by the hospital again for another quick check on Sam before she went home. When she walked into the intensive care unit, Sam was sleeping. The nurse on duty motioned for her to come in, so she walked in and sat in the chair next to his bed. As soon as she reached over and grabbed Sam's hand, he slowly opened his left eye.

"Hello, Sam," Kate whispered. "I just stopped by to see how you were doing. Everyone down at the nursing home has been asking about you all day. I can only stay a few minutes. I have to go home and get Josh and Billy. We're meeting a group of about 25 people at the foot of the plateau at four o'clock. We're going to start searching for your gold chain."

Sam slowly held up his hand to motion Kate to come closer. He wanted to whisper something.

"Ten days," Sam whispered, in a faint raspy voice.

"Ten days for what, Sam? What's going to happen in ten days?"

"Santa," Sam whispered. "Find my gold chain, please."

"Christmas, in ten days it … it *will* be Christmas. Is that what you're trying to tell me, Sam?"

He nodded his head and then motioned for Kate to come closer again.

"Find the chain ... by Christmas Eve, Kate, by Christmas Eve, please."

"Christmas Eve," Kate repeated. "You want us to find your gold chain by Christmas Eve? Why, Sam? Why by Christmas Eve?"

"Santa will come for me at midnight, Kate."

Kate sat back down in the chair and looked over at him.

"How do you know this, Sam? How do you know Santa will come to get you on Christmas Eve? Are you telling me that if we can find your gold chain, Santa will know that you're here and he'll come to get you?"

Sam nodded again. Kate just sat back in the chair not knowing what to say. Suddenly she stood up.

"Sam, I have to leave now. I have to meet up with the group, I'll see you tomorrow."

As she reached for the door handle, she stopped and turned around.

"Sam, we're going to find your gold chain. It might not be tonight or tomorrow night, but we're going to find it! On Christmas Eve night, you're going to be standing up on the plateau waiting for Santa to take you back to the North Pole."

Kate didn't realize what she had just said to Sam until she walked out of the room.

"I can't believe I just promised him that," Kate whispered to herself. "If we don't find that chain, I'll never be able to forgive myself."

John was closing the garage door just as Kate pulled into the driveway.

"Kate, I asked Josh about that giant pine tree today. He said there isn't a giant pine tree up by the cabin, just a bunch of smaller ones. He said there wasn't a single tree in that area any taller than the highest peak of our house."

"But Sam *said* it was real close to the cabin. It has to be there," Kate demanded, as she rushed into the house.

"Josh, is it true what your father just told me about the giant pine tree? There isn't a giant tree up by the cabin?"

"That's right, Mom. All that's up there is a bunch of little trees. Maybe somebody chopped it down."

"No," John said, as he walked up behind Kate. "They've never done any logging up on the plateau."

"Then maybe it got old and fell down," Josh said. A couple years ago when Billy and I were up in the hills, we saw where this huge tree had fallen down and crushed everything in its path, right down to the ground. It was all rotted and mushy."

Kate turned around and looked at John.

"Maybe that's what happened to that giant pine tree," Kate said. "It's been what, twelve years since Sam moved into the nursing home? That tree could have fallen down within that time. We might be able to find the chain on the ground where it fell."

"That's only if he lost it in that particular tree, Kate. That chain could be stuck on top of any one of a thousand trees that surround the plateau all through those hills."

"But it won't be, John. If, indeed, that giant pine tree really did fall, then that's where we're going to find Wendell's gold chain. We all have to believe that."

After they gathered a few pairs of gloves, the rakes and the shovels, they jumped into the car and headed for the plateau. Driving down the dirt road, toward Millie's house, they could see the long line of cars already parked on either side. They ended up parking about ten cars back. As they walked, Kate could see a large group gathered together close by the log bridge. Also, she noticed that there were twice as many people waiting for them as there were at the meeting last night. Kate quickly spotted Claire, Bob and Billy with their gloves on and rakes in hand, ready to get to work.

"Hello, everybody," Kate shouted. "I thought *we'd* be the first ones here tonight, but you all beat us to it. I see that a lot of you brought friends along, thanks, that's terrific! We're going to need all the help we can get. Does everyone know why we're here? Did your friends share the story about Wendell with you?"

They all gave the "yes" nod.

"Ok, then. Josh, why don't you and Billy get up front so you two can show us the way to the site of the cabin."

Single file, they followed the boys across the old logging bridge and up the old narrow logging trail that, splits-off, to the plateau. The trek across the tall-grassed, weed-ridden plateau with its pounded-down path was like walking through a maze. The path led to a small grove of pine trees that grew along some of the remains of the stone wall that used to support the cabin. When they reached the cabin they formed a circle around the boys.

Billy and Josh quickly weaved their way through the piles of rotted wood to get to the dirt floor of the cabin. They wanted to show off the large **W** that was carved on the footboard of Wendell's bed. Also, they held up other things, such as clothing, eating utensils, some partially rotted wood carvings and a half dozen other items. Then they pointed out the rock wall they tore down that lay scattered across the cabin's dirt floor. The back part of the wall was still intact, so everyone was able to get a good view of where the chest of journals had been entombed for all those years. Everyone was very impressed that Josh and Billy were able to remove all that wood to find as much as they did in such a short time. The praise got a little embarrassing for the boys when everyone started clapping and carrying on.

As they climbed out from the rubble and melded back in with the rest of the group, Josh and Billy started explaining what Sam had told them about where the cabin was in relation to the giant pine tree. This would give them an idea of what direction the tree was so they could begin their search. From where the group was standing, the entire area around the cabin was completely overgrown with tall weeds and a dozen or so 15 to 20 foot high pine trees. There were also thick batches of vines growing wild on just about every-thing in sight.

They all stood still and carefully scanned the surroundings. It was definitely overwhelming. It was going to take a lot more work than they had anticipated.

"It's going to take at least a week to clear all this brush away before we can even *start* to think about looking for that gold chain," Paul Adder yelled out, from the center of the group. Paul, Matilda's husband, was one of the half dozen lawyers in town that volunteered.

"Paul's right," said John. "We're going to need more than rakes and shovels to clear this away. We're going to need heavy duty hand shears and hand saws to cut down some of these smaller trees. I suggest we try locating the remains of this tree first and start from there. Then when we come back up here tomorrow, we'll start cutting away all this overgrowth so we can start searching around on the ground."

"I'm off all day tomorrow," shouted Jerry Fields.

"So am I," said Butch Conley. "There's about five of us up here that work the split-shift over at Saunders Mill, and tomorrow's our day off. I can't speak for the rest of these guys, but I have some equipment at the house that can clear most of this brush away in a hurry. Now, I can be up here first thing in the morning, but I'll need a couple of hands to help me with the equipment."

All five of Jerry's coworkers quickly raised their hands and assured everyone that they'd be here bright and early to help Jerry. Suddenly everyone started milling around asking what they should start doing, how much area they'd have to clear, and what to bring tomorrow night. Kate and Claire were in the middle of it all, trying desperately to answer everyone's questions. During the ruckus, John and Bob ventured off through the brush in search of any remains of the giant pine. Billy and Josh followed close behind and eventually pushed their way to the front. They still felt like they should be in charge. After all, they did find the chest with the journals that started this whole thing. Suddenly, Billy yelled out, "I found it! I found it!" Josh, Bob, and John just about trampled over each other trying to get to the spot where Billy was.

There it was, right before their very eyes. The massive pine tree looked like it fell to the ground several years before, because the branches were drooping down to the ground. There wasn't a single pine needle still attached to any of the branches. The tree, even though it was lying on its side, was more than four feet high from the ground. Hundreds of vines grew thick from the ground and covered most branches along the length of the tree.

"I think this is the biggest pine tree I've ever seen," John said, as he grabbed onto a couple of branches to climb up top.

"Hey, everyone," John yelled, as he appeared to be standing in mid-air from where the rest of the group was standing. "Guess what Billy just found?"

"The giant pine tree," Kate cheered. "Is that what you're standing on?"

"Sure is. Looks like that Sam of yours was right. This is the biggest pine tree I've ever seen. From up here, you can see how truly massive this tree really was. The vines have just about taken the whole thing over, though. But we're lucky its winter time, because the leaves have fallen-off from most of these vines, otherwise, it'd be almost impossible to see through all these branches."

Billy and Josh climbed up onto the tree and stood next to Josh's dad. They immediately started walking toward the top end of the tree while peeking over its sides, as they began searching for the gold chain. Smaller pine trees had grown close together on either side of the giant pine and their branches hung *well* over the top. The boys had to *continually* push them aside as they worked their way forward. Josh quickly learned that it was easier to get on his hands and knees and crawl than to chance getting slapped in the face by a pine branch when Billy released one in front of him.

"Squat down, Billy," Josh suggested, as he continued to crawl and look down through the dead branches. "This way you won't have to keep pushing those branches out of your way."

"Oh, yeah, good idea," Billy said, as he got on his knees and crawled just in front of Josh.

After a few minutes, about a dozen other kids were crawling up and down the length of the tree hoping to be the first one to spot the gold chain. They looked like a bunch of kids hunting for Easter eggs. Still, with the new pine tree branches and the thick vines blocking their view, it was nearly impossible to do a thorough search. The gold chain was small in comparison to the massive size of the pine tree, so it wasn't going to be easy to locate.

On the ground, everyone was branching off in all directions to conduct their own separate searches. An hour later it was getting too dark to see, so everyone began making their way across the plateau and down to the log bridge. After they gathered back into a group at the bottom of the plateau, Kate thanked everyone for their help and said she looked forward to seeing them the next day again about the same time. She also reminded everyone to bring gloves, hand shears, hedge shears, saws, and anything else they had at home that would help cut down the brush and clear away the vines.

Chapter Fifteen

_T_he next day John woke up with a sore back from all the climb-ing around he did on the giant pine tree.

As Kate sat at the kitchen table adding to her list of things to take up to the plateau, she heard John moaning and groaning as he came shuffling down the stairs. She quickly got up to pour him a cup of coffee.

"I can't believe I let you talk me into another one of your _save the world_ projects, Kate," John complained, as he walked toward the counter to reach for the freshly filled cup of coffee Kate was holding for him.

"Wait just one second there, John Lewis," Kate snapped, setting the cup of coffee down and scooting it behind her in protest while she leaned up against the counter. "When was the last time I asked you to volunteer for something that didn't turn out to be a worth-while cause?"

"I don't know," John answered, as he lurched for the cup of cof-fee.

"No, you don't, mister! You're not getting this cup of coffee until you've answered the question. And by the way, this is probably the best pot of coffee I have ever made in my entire life."

"Okay, you win ... I have never worked on one of your _causes_ that didn't pan out. They were all worth it. You're the best."

"That was good. Now try saying it *without* the sarcasm!"

"I'm sorry, babe. My back's killing me from all that climbing around on that tree last night. I guess I'm just getting too old for that kind of stuff. As for your projects, you know that I never mind helping you out with them, and they are *always* for a good cause. You're a saint, and I really do mean that."

"Well," Kate said, "that was a little better. Even though this *is* Josh and Billy's project, I do take it very personal. Here's your coffee ... enjoy. I'm going upstairs to take a quick shower before I go to work. Take a look at that pad of paper I left on the kitchen table. It's a list of stuff we'll need tonight, check it to see if I forgot anything," she yelled over her shoulder, as she continued walking down the hallway.

After work that night, Kate drove over to the hospital to visit Sam before heading home. As she opened the door, she noticed that Sam was sound asleep. The nurse said he hadn't eaten anything or said much all day. But she quickly assured Kate that such behavior was completely normal for someone who'd been through as much as he had in the last couple days.

"He should start coming around any day now, and by week's end, he should be talking and eating just fine."

Kate thanked the nurse and left the room. When she got to the house, the boys were all ready to go and waiting for her at the end of the driveway.

"Where's your father's car, Josh?" Kate asked, as she drove into the driveway.

"Dad and Mr. Phillips drove it over to the plateau."

"Why didn't he wait for us? I came home early today so we could all go up there together. Do you know what time they left?"

"He left right after you went to work this morning. He said he was going over to pick up Billy's dad and drive up to the plateau to get an early start."

"Did he say anything to you about his back hurting?" Kate questioned, looking somewhat suspicious.

"No," Josh replied.

"Josh, I hope you grow up to be just like your father. He's a little sneaky at times, but he's a good man," Kate said, as she rushed into the house to change her clothes.

Kate, Claire, and the boys arrived at Millie's dirt road an hour earlier than the previous day and were able to get within a few car lengths from the base of the plateau. The crowd from last night hadn't showed up yet, so there were only a couple cars there besides John's.

When they reached the top of the plateau, heading toward the cabin, Claire spotted Bob and John working on top of the giant pine tree. They were cutting away vines and tossing them aside while others were busily clearing the area around the tree. As they stood at the front of the cabin, they could almost see the entire length of the giant pine tree as it lay on its side. They couldn't believe how much of the area had been cleared away.

"This is how it must have looked when Sam lived here," said Kate, as she stood with her arms folded talking about what a great job the men had done in such a short time.

When she moved closer to the tree, John saw her coming and climbed down to greet her.

"Sore back, huh?" Kate said, as she smiled and threw her arms around his neck.

About that time Bob, Jerry, Butch and the rest of the guys stopped what they were doing to take a break.

"You have all done an incredible job today," Kate said. "This doesn't even look like the same place anymore! I hope everyone who came up here to help out last night will show up again tonight, because now we can finally start searching. I'm so proud of you guys. Thanks for taking the day off and doing all this."

Within the hour, over sixty people showed up to join in the search. The story of Sam's real identity as *Wendell, the Christmas elf* had continued to spread throughout the town.

The boys and their moms ended up spending most of their time supervising and answering questions other than doing any actual searching for Wendell's chain.

The next day at the nursing home brought a total bombardment of questions from the nurses, the doctors, and some of the patients who'd become good friends with Sam over the years. Some were in total disbelief, while others said they weren't as surprised when they heard the news of Sam's real identity. They always felt that Sam was different, in a special kind of way, which made him unique. Even though he mostly kept to himself, he was always very friendly to everyone.

"He never asked for help and never complained about any-thing," Edna Tripp, the head nurse added. "I always thought it was odd, though, that a retired furniture maker would have all those little carvings of people making toys, reindeer, and Santa Claus pulling a sleigh. He brought boxes packed full of those things when he first moved in here. I never saw him do any actual carving, but I do recall asking him about them one day. He told me how much he used to enjoy carving and about all the different things he had carved over the years. But, once his hands got so bad with the arthritis, he said he was forced to give it up."

During their lunch break that day, Kate hinted to Claire that she was thinking about taking the rest of the week off to avoid all the distractions and questions about Sam at work so she could concen-trate on looking for the chain. Claire thought that was a great idea. After work that night, Claire went to the hospital with Kate to check on Sam.

"Sam's pretty much the same as he was yesterday," said the nurse on duty, as they slowly walked into the room. "He hasn't been able to eat solid food since the stroke. The doctor suggested that we just leave him alone. He said the sleep would do him a world of good. The doctor came in an hour ago and checked him; said he was doing fine. I guess he'll just have to remain on the feeding tube until he can start eating on his own."

"Could we have a few moments alone with him, please?" Kate asked, in that motherly tone.

"Sure," replied the nurse. "I'll just take my break now. You know where the break room is. Just buzz me if something comes up. I should be back in about twenty minutes."

"Thank you so much," Kate said.

As soon as Kate walked over to the far side of Sam's bed and sat down on the chair, Sam opened his eyes.

"Good afternoon, ladies."

"Sam!" Kate jumped, "You're awake. You scared the heck out of me."

"Didn't mean to do that," Sam apologized. "I've been laying awake here for most of the day. Just haven't been in the mood to talk to anyone until I heard you two come in. How are the boys doing? What about the search; did you find anything yet?"

"Nothing yet, Sam," Kate replied. "You sure are full of questions today."

"I guess it's just all the excitement; you're all up there working so hard trying to find my gold chain. That's all," Sam confessed.

"I know Sam," Kate said. "But I do have *some* good news. Last night we had over sixty people come out to help. And then yesterday morning seven men took off work and spent the whole day cutting down the weeds and vines before we could even get near that giant pine tree. By the way Sam, that giant pine tree of yours is now laying on the ground."

"You cut it down?" Sam questioned.

"No, no, Sam. It fell down by itself. Josh thought the stump may have rotted and the wind finally just blew it over."

"That used to be such a beautiful place up there," Sam said, as he began to reminisce. "I used to spend every Saturday morning tending to the yard, picking weeds, watering the flowers, and working in the garden. Millie would always come up to help me do all those things. Then we would just let nature take its course and watch it grow. We had tomatoes, cucumbers, green beans and lettuce. We grew all kinds of stuff. We even grew a couple rows of pumpkins and watermelons. I remember she'd always bring me fresh vegetables from her family's garden; things that I didn't grow in mine. Her dad grew the sweetest tasting corn around. I always made sure I built her folks a nice piece of furniture for Christmas, you know, for being so nice to me throughout the year and all. They were poor folk, and I always did what I could for them. After all, they did let me stay in that cabin all those years. They were good people. After they passed on, I felt obligated to watch out after Millie. At least up until it was time for me to move into the nursing home. Millie was a little slow, you know, in the head, but she was a good person, and I knew she would be able to take care of herself once I went away and ..."

Suddenly, the door opened and the nurse walked back into the room. The girls said their goodbyes to Sam and left the room. For the next couple nights the amount of people showing up to participate in the search for Wendell's chain had doubled. By Sunday, there were over a 150 people searching more than a 300 foot diameter area around the tree.

The weather for the last few days stayed clear and remained in the mid to high 40's, which was unseasonably warm for that time of year. But that was about to change. The temperature had been dropping a degree an hour since nine o'clock that morning, and snow was predicted within the next couple days. Normally, everyone in town would be wishing for a white Christmas, but not this year ... not until they found Wendell's gold chain.

"Kate, did you happen to catch the weather report today?" Claire questioned.

"No, I didn't, and please don't tell me they're predicting snow. I don't think I could handle that."

"Sorry, Kate," Claire said, "but they are. They're predicting snow within the next couple days, with a big storm forecasted for Christmas day. So, if we're going to find that gold chain of Wendell's, we need to find it soon."

"We'll find it, Claire. We *have* to. That chain has got to be in this area somewhere. Any minute now someone is going to stand up and yell out loud with that gold chain dangling from their fingers tips."

"I hope so, Kate. For Sam's sake … I hope so."

"You know, Claire, when I talked to Josh yesterday, he said he wished that he and Billy had never found that chest. He feels so bad for Sam right now because everyone's been building his hopes up about finding his chain. I tried convincing him that we all feel the way he does, but he said we can't possibly feel as bad as he and Billy … they're the ones who found the chest."

"I know," Claire said, "Billy talked to me about this yesterday as well. I guess the boys must have talked about this before they approached us with it. But you know Kate, ever since we found out that Sam is Wendell, and that he really *is* an elf, I've been thinking about it nearly every waking hour. I don't think I've had a decent night's sleep since this whole thing started. So, the boys are not alone in this; you and I are carrying around a lot of this guilt as well."

As the sun dipped below the horizon, still hidden behind the clouds, daylight quickly faded, and the temperature steadily dropped. It was nearly impossible to see the ground, and several people started complaining that they could no longer feel their fingers or toes. Before long, everyone decided to call it quits for the night. Kate stood and watched as the continuous stream of people steadily disappeared into the darkness as they walked across the plateau. She knew that, as soon as they got down to the road, they'd make haste to find their cars so they could get back to their cozy-warm homes.

"You know, Josh, I'll bet you that not long after Wendell fell onto that tree a big bird plucked up that chain from one of the branches and flew off with it. It probably flew all the way to the coast and dropped it off into the Atlantic Ocean," Billy said, as he and Josh walked toward the old log bridge.

"I don't know," Josh replied. "I hate to think that something like that actually happened, but I guess it's possible. Birds do like things that are shiny and gold *is* about as shiny as you can get."

Kate and Claire walked quietly behind and heard every word the boys were saying.

"Is that true?" Kate asked, as she looked over at John.

"I'm afraid so, babe. All birds like shiny objects. That's why they like flying over our nice shiny car every time I wash it and leave that not so pleasant surprise for me to clean up," joked John.

"This isn't a good time to be kidding around, John. If a bird really did take that chain, we may never find it, and Sam will never turn back into Wendell."

"I think the chances of a bird taking that chain are probably a million to one," Bob said, as he chuckled and put his arm around Claire's shoulder. "Don't let John kid you like that, Kate. Birds only *like* shiny things. They rarely pick them up and fly away with them, especially something as heavy as a gold chain."

"Thanks Bob. That makes me feel a little better," Kate said, as she poked John in the ribs with her elbow.

Chapter Sixteen

*T*uesday brought sporadic snow flurries, which fortunately only amounted to a light dusting. But the temperature steadily dropped and was expected to be in the teens by mid-day, which made it difficult to remain focused on cutting down weeds and raking when your fingers were numb from the cold.

Soon after Josh and Billy were out of school for the day, they made their way up to the plateau to start gathering rocks to build fire pits. This was an idea that their dads came up with. Not only did this keep everyone warm during their time on the plateau, it also eliminated the growing piles of brush and twigs that were getting in the way.

Josh and Billy happily volunteered to gather wood throughout the night to keep the fires burning. The fires also gave off a tremendous amount of light that lit up most of the area to help make the searching efforts less of a burden. Nearly everyone continued working as long as they could. It was well after ten before they all decided to finally call it a night.

Wednesday morning arrived and Kate's trusty old alarm clock began hammering away. With her eyes still closed, she reached over to her night stand and shut it off. "Ah, silence," she whispered, as she continued to lie in bed with the sheets pulled up over her head. She didn't even want to think about getting up. It seemed like, for the last week or so, she found herself getting pulled into a routine that was starting to wear heavily on her: The hours at the nursing home, visiting Sam at the hospital, crawling around half the night up on the plateau looking for a needle in a haystack. Then, in the midst of all that, there was the constant worry about whether they were ever actually going to find the gold chain at all. Total exhaustion was rapidly approaching, and Kate knew it.

John had been awake long before the alarm went off, but he quietly stayed in bed contemplating how he could be of more help to the boys. He knew for a fact what Josh and Billy had been going through over the past few weeks, and it worried him to see them stressed-out all the time. Lately, without the boys or the girls knowing about it, he and Bob had been spreading the word about Wendell all around town, trying to recruit more people to come out and help. They even made posters and passed them out to all the store owners so they could hang them in their storefront windows.

Suddenly, Kate yawned and stretched, then turned on her side to face John.

"Good morning, dear," she said, yawning again and gently easing her head onto his chest. "Please tell me we don't have to get up today. I don't think I can find the strength."

"Sorry, babe, I have to get up now, and so do you. We have to get ready for work."

"I knew you were going to say that," she said, moving back to her side of the bed. "Just for that, you go make the coffee this morning."

"I was on my way," he replied, as he leaned over and kissed her on the forehead.

"And make it strong," Kate yelled, as she yanked the covers back up over her head.

When she finally got up and out of bed, she walked into the kitchen and noticed Josh sitting at the kitchen table with his arms crossed and looking rather depressed.

"Why the sad face, Josh?" she asked, automatically touching his forehead to see if he was running a fever.

"He doesn't want to go to school today," John said. "Apparently, some of the kids at school have been making fun of him and Billy and their friends that have been helping out, with all this Wendell-the-elf business."

"Don't worry, Josh, when we find Wendell's gold chain and Santa Claus comes to get him, we'll have the last laugh. There are a lot of adults in this town that are doing the same thing to everyone who is helping us, too. But soon the whole town will experience the magic of Christmas, right before their very eyes, just like we did that night at the nursing home. Josh, just keep thinking about that night ... that night when Wendell showed us the truth."

"Let's hope we're right," whispered John, as he walked past Kate. "Oh yeah, I almost forgot. There's another article about Wendell in the morning paper."

She immediately grabbed her coffee and sat down to read it.

"It's right there on the front page, Mom," Josh said, as he pointed it out to her.

When she read it out loud, it sounded more like a genuine plea for help than a tongue-in-cheek story about an elf.

With only a couple days left before Christmas, while everyone is out doing their last minute shopping, or decorating their houses and Christmas trees, getting ready for the big day, let us take some time to help those that have dedicated their lives to make this town what it is today. So make an effort to go out and get involved before it's too late. I think most of you know what I'm talking about. The search for Wendell's gold chain continues up on the plateau, and there are only two days left. Please help get Wendell back home. If you're interested in helping, please contact Josh Lewis or Billy Phillips.

"What a nice article," Kate said, as she looked over at Josh. "Oh, Josh, so this is the reason you don't want to go to school today, because you think some kids are going to see this article."

"Yeah, once they read that article they're really going to make fun of Billy and me."

"Like I said before, Josh, we'll be the last ones laughing, not those bullies at school."

As soon as Josh left the kitchen, he went upstairs to get ready for school. Kate immediately went to the phone to call Claire about the newspaper article. Claire was just as surprised as Kate was, but neither one of them had any idea who was behind it.

"What are we going to do if half the town comes out to help?" Claire asked; sounding a little panicked over the phone. "I'm sure that since it's so close to Christmas, people with even half a heart are going to want to do what they can to help us find that chain."

"Claire, get a hold of your self. Everything's going to be just fine. There's plenty to do for the folks around town. Just in case you didn't notice, that's a pretty big area up there. There's room for the whole town to help in the search. If more people volunteer to help, we'll just have to expand the search to cover more area. The more help we have, the better our chances will be of finding that gold chain."

"You're right, Kate, that chain could be anywhere up there. I guess more people *would* make sense, Oh, it's getting late and I'm still not ready for work yet. I'll talk to you in a little while."

About thirty minutes later, as Kate was walking out the side door to the driveway, the phone rang.

"Oh, no," Kate said, as she walked back into the house to pick up the phone. "This can't be someone calling to volunteer already."

"Hello," Kate said, hoping it would be Claire at the other end.

"Kate, this is Martha Wilson from the corner market on Main Street. I read that article about Wendell in the paper this morning and how your son Josh and his friend Billy have been heading up the search for his gold chain. I think it's just a wonderful way to get people into the Christmas spirit. It reminds me of how we used to do things in the old days, you know, helping each other out and all, especially the needy folks. Anyway, my grandson goes to school with your boy Josh, and he tells me that you had more than 150 volunteers the last couple of nights. Well, my husband and I talked about it and we would like to know if it would be all right if we made sandwiches for everyone. It'll be our way of pitching in and helping out the best way we can."

"Well, that would be just wonderful, Martha, I don't know what to say."

"No need to say anything, dear. It'll be our pleasure. We just want to help. I'll just have my deli girl Rebecca and a few of our bag boys meet you in front of Millie's house about four?"

"You know Millie?" Kate asked.

"Oh, yes, I've known Millie ever since *I* was a little girl. She can't get around much anymore like she used to, you know, on account of the bad hips and all. So we make weekly deliveries out to her."

"Well, thank you very much, Martha. We surely do appreciate it, and I'll be sure to be at Millie's at four o'clock sharp."

Kate couldn't wait to get down to the nursing home to tell Claire the news. She smiled as she left the house.

Soon after Kate walked into the nursing home, she located Claire and told her the good news about Mrs. Wilson from the corner market. After several minutes of talking about the article, the number of sandwiches the deli was going to make and the fact that Mrs. Wilson from the deli actually knew who Millie was, it was time to start work. They split up and began making their rounds, checking in on all their patients. Today, most of them wanted to know the details of how the search was going, while others were just interested in how Sam was doing at the hospital. All the questions were starting to wear on the girls, so several times during the day they would sneak off to the nurse's lounge to enjoy a little peace and quiet over a hot cup of coffee.

Kate was looking forward to visiting Sam after work. Josh had talked to her about asking Sam some more questions about the night he fell. He wanted to know if Sam had his chain protected by an overcoat, or did he just have a vest on where one end of his chain connected through a buttonhole. He really wanted to find out if there was any possibility that his chain could have gotten hung-up on Santa's sleigh. It may not make any difference, but if there were little to no chance at all that his gold chain was still on the sleigh, then it had to either be in the tree or on the ground. That would make Josh feel a whole lot better about the search. Shortly after noon, Kate and Claire's second-shift counterparts came strolling into the room where Kate was looking in on a patient.

"Well, good afternoon, Barbara," Kate said. "What are you doing here so early? Your shift doesn't start for another three hours."

"Not today, Kate."

"Excuse me," Kate said.

"I read that article in the newspaper this morning. How on earth do you and Claire find enough time in the day to do all the things you do? I have a hard enough time keeping up with just my nursing duties. But you two have poor Sam to deal with, all those volunteers helping you up in the woods, and now the press. That's way too much for two people, Kate. So, here's the deal. After I read that article, I called all the second-shift girls and asked if they'd be willing to do some volunteering. Of course, they all said they couldn't because they had to work. Then I suggested that we could help out by coming in a few hours early for the next few days. They jumped at the opportunity. So, that's why I'm here."

"Barbara, I don't know what to say. I can't believe you're doing this."

"It's the Christmas spirit, Kate, and Josh and Billy are the reason it's spreading around town so fast. Go on and tell Claire and the rest of the day-shifters that they've been relieved of duty, and go find that gold chain."

Kate ran out of the room and immediately informed the others. Then she and Claire hurried off to get Josh and Billy so they could talk to Sam before heading back up to the plateau. He was sound asleep when they walked into his room, but as soon as he heard Kate talking to the nurse, he woke up.

"Good afternoon, ladies and gentlemen," he said, as a small smile formed on the left side of his face. "How's the search coming along?"

"Fine, Sam," Josh replied, as everyone pulled a chair up close to the bed.

"Sam," Josh spoke, "I was hoping you could tell me more about what happened that night you fell from Santa's sleigh. I'd like to know how your watch and chain were attached to your clothing."

"That was a long time ago Josh. Let me think for a moment. I always kept my watch in my left pants pocket and attached the chain to the second buttonhole from the bottom of my vest, just in case it slipped out of my hand while I checked the time. Back at the North Pole, I must have checked the time a hundred times a day. Time is crucial when you're under a tight schedule, as we were in the workshop. Every second is an important one."

"What about an overcoat, Sam? Did you have an overcoat on that night?"

"Oh, yes. Any time an elf travels with Santa on his sleigh, he has to dress for the coldest of cold temperatures. A thick overcoat with a hood is standard elf attire for such a trip, plus boots, thick mittens, and a scarf."

"Then there's no way that your gold chain could have gotten caught on the sleigh," Billy yelled out, as he proudly looked around the room. "The chain must have come off when you fell through all those pine branches. That's the only thing that makes sense, Sam."

Sam sat there for the longest time, with the strangest look on his face.

"What's the matter?" Kate asked Sam, as she reached over and tapped him on the shoulder.

"Oh, I'm sorry. I ... I was just trying to recall some memory of what happened that night. I vaguely remember the buttons on my overcoat tearing off and flying through the air as they whisked by my head. It was like everything was in slow motion. But I definitely remember falling down through the branches. That's when pieces of my overcoat were tearing off. That's about the last thing I could remember. When I woke up, I was lying in about two feet of snow, looking up at the tree. It was daytime then ... and I was alone. It was difficult to move at first. I remember being all banged up from the fall and having this terrible headache. I guess I was lucky to be in one piece. Elves may live forever, but they can still get hurt. After I was able to start moving around, I reached into my pocket to pull out my watch. That's when I discovered the chain was gone. My heart felt like it broke in two. It felt like I'd lost my best friend ... my lifeline ... my way home."

"Sam," Josh said, as he looked at him with determination in his eyes, "with what you've told me so far, it sounds like that chain must still be attached somewhere on that giant pine tree. It probably got caught on a branch when your overcoat tore off."

The room grew silent for a few moments. Sam didn't know what to say. What Josh just said, made perfect sense to him.

"We have to leave now, Sam," Kate said, "I think we have a better idea of where we should be searching for your gold chain now."

The boys, along with Kate and Claire were ecstatic when they left the hospital room.

"That was simple," Josh said boastfully, as Kate unlocked the door to the car. "I can't believe we didn't ask Sam all those questions before. We might have already found his chain by now, and Sam would have already turned back into Wendell."

"At least we know now," Kate said. "Oh, Claire, don't forget, we have to meet Rebecca from the deli in front of Millie's house at four o'clock to pick up all those sandwiches."

Chapter Seventeen

$\mathcal{J}$ ohn and Bob were able to leave work for the day by 11:00 a.m. This gave them an early start to clear more of the brush from around the upper half of the fallen pine before too many people got in their way. The lower half of the tree had previously been stripped of most of its vines, and several people had already conducted an exhaustive search all the way down to the underbrush.

As soon as the boys walked out the front doors of their school, they spotted their moms parked in front waiting to pick them up. After a quick stop home to change, they drove down through town toward the dirt road. When Kate left the pavement and drove toward the plateau, she noticed that John's car was already there.

"Mom," Josh yelled, "that looks like our car. Dad must be up on the plateau already."

"Sure looks like it," Kate said, as she glanced suspiciously over at Claire. "He told me this morning that he wouldn't be home from work until after three."

As soon as Kate opened her door and stepped out, she could see Millie sitting in her rocker on the front porch. But she was just sitting there, no rocking back and forth, no friendly hello, just staring up at the hills as if she were waiting for something. As they walked toward the log bridge, Josh turned around several times to see if she had moved. The last time he looked, she stood up and disappeared into the house.

"That old lady gives me the creeps," Josh whispered, as he walked across the bridge along side of Billy.

"That's not very nice, Josh," Kate lectured. "What did I tell you about respecting your elders?"

"Sorry, Mom, but she's always staring at us when we go by. It's creepy."

"She's probably just daydreaming, Josh."

As they walked along the path toward the cabin, they could hear rustling of branches and other commotion coming from the direction of the giant pine tree. As they moved in closer, they could see John and Bob working toward the top end of the tree. Kate wasn't at all that surprised, as she stood silent and watched as John pulled vines away from the tree while Bob broke them loose with an axe.

"So," Kate yelled, "you guys took off from work early again today I see?"

"Oh, hi, guys!" Bob answered, as he nudged John, "We didn't expect to see you so early, as he rested the axe against the tree. "Another couple of hours and John and I should have all these vines cleared away from the entire upper half of this tree."

"Good," said Josh. "Then we'll be able to search around all these branches."

"So, how did you girls get off so early today?"

"Night shift came in early today and told us to leave. As a matter of fact, they'll be coming in early for the next three days to work an extended shift just so we can get an early start up here. They figured since they couldn't volunteer to work up here, they would just relieve us so we could get an earlier start."

"Well, isn't that funny," Bob replied.

"Why do you say that?" Claire questioned.

"Well, the same thing happened to me today. About ten o'clock this morning. My boss called me into his office and told me that after I was finished with the project I was working on, to just take the rest of the week off. He said this would give me more time to search for Wendell's chain. That surprised the heck out of me. He usually turns into a scrooge this time of year. But he said pretty much the same thing. He just wanted to do his part to help."

"What about you, John?" Kate asked, as she stood with her arms folded. "What's your excuse for being up here so early?"

"It's got to be that newspaper article. My boss let me loose around ten, also. I didn't even realize he knew anything about Wendell and his gold chain. And there's more. He told me that during work today he was going to start recruiting as many guys and gals from around the factory as he could to come up here to help out after work. I'm telling you, it seems that everybody in town is on this magical Christmas kick, and the closer we get to Christmas Eve, the more surprises there are."

"I think we're all in for a big night tonight," Claire announced. "Kate and I have to meet the deli girl and some of the bag boys from the corner market down at Millie's house at four o'clock. They're making sandwiches for everyone who's helping out tonight."

"How did you finagle that one?" John asked.

"It wasn't me. Mr. and Mrs. Wilson, the owners of the corner market, read that article this morning and asked if they could pitch in by feeding everyone dinner tonight."

Before John and Bob went back to stripping the rest of the vines from the tree, they scrounged around for firewood to rebuild the fires that they, along with the boys, had made the previous night. Most of the vines they'd already removed from the tree were old and dead, so Bob decided to chop them into three foot long pieces and start a pile big enough to last the night.

"Hey, boys, come over here and grab some of these vines we've cut up, and start making piles next to the fire pits."

John started the fires while the girls grabbed their rakes and started clearing the weeds from around the giant pine.

"That chain has to be on this tree somewhere, Billy," Josh said, as he threw branches onto the pile. "The way Sam described his fall this is the only logical place it could be."

"You're right, Josh. There's no question about that. I just hope it's not underneath this tree, because if it is, we'll never be able to get to it before Christmas Eve."

"That's the first thing I thought about when we discovered this tree," Josh replied. "Let's just hope that isn't the case."

Around three o'clock, Kate heard voices moving toward her from across the plateau.

"Here they come," Kate shouted.

The first ones to arrive were the day nurses from Kate's work, along with their kids and some friends. Behind them were a mix of new faces and a large number of returns from last night. Everyone seemed better prepared this time with all their rakes, lawn shears, and blankets. Others carried grocery bags full of snacks and Thermoses. Several of them brought lawn chairs so they'd have a place to sit as they warmed themselves by the fire.

"Look at all these people," Claire said, as she stopped raking to watch them file past the collapsed cabin. "They sure did come better prepared tonight. We should have thought about bringing some lawn chairs and blankets up with us."

"The thought never crossed my mind," Kate replied.

John's boss, Tom Brockway, came strolling around the collapsed cabin wearing a big old thick jacket and carrying a couple of kerosene lanterns.

"How's it going up here, John?" Tom shouted, as he set the lanterns down on the ground and began introducing himself and several of his employees who came with him to all the others. "Looks like its going to be another cold one tonight. Anyway, tell us where to start, John, we came up here to do some work."

Over the next two hours, people kept coming. They brought more flashlights, lanterns, blankets and Thermoses full of hot coffee and cocoa. They even brought more chairs. After a while, there were so many people working on the plateau, Stub Hammond and his sons, along with several of the other kids, had to gather more rocks to build two additional fire pits. The two they previously built weren't big enough to keep everyone warm.

Around seven o'clock, while Big John Jacobs was searching the upper half of the giant pine, he found a piece of red material wrapped around a branch, with a single gold button attached. He immediately shouted for Josh and Billy to come over to take a look. Everyone up on the plateau heard Big John yell, and they instantly stopped what they were doing and rushed over to where he was working. Josh and Billy immediately thought that Big John had found Wendell's chain.

"I'm sorry," Big John apologized, as he saw the excitement on the boys' faces, "I didn't mean to get everyone so excited. It's just that I found this red piece of material and this button and thought it might be something of importance. That's all."

As Josh pushed a couple branches out of the way to get a closer look, he began to smile. "Billy, look at this, this must be one of the buttons from Wendell's overcoat. Just like he said back at the nursing home, you know, when he told us the story about the night he fell from the sleigh. Remember … he said he saw the buttons flying past him as he fell through the branches. This has to be one of those buttons."

The red material, along with the button, appeared to be growing out from the tree within the crevice of a branch encased in pine sap. The button was definitely gold, and it had a faint impression of a snowflake on its face. There wasn't any doubt as to whom it belonged.

"Listen, everyone," Billy shouted, as he tried to calm everybody down. "Big John just found a piece of Wendell's coat, and it has a gold button still attached. This is the first real piece of proof we've found so far. We're getting closer everyone, let's keep on searching. Wendell's gold chain has got to be somewhere around in this area."

Suddenly, a line started to form along the length of the giant pine tree as everyone pulled back the branches to catch a quick glimpse of the button before they resumed their work. This would be the one thing to keep them motivated for the rest of the night.

Kate walked over to John and leaned her head against his shoulder. "Why haven't we been able to find that chain yet, honey? I'm getting so tired, and I know the boys are exhausted. I'm not sure how much longer everyone is going to be able to keep this up."

"We'll find it. Kate. Besides, that piece of material with the button attached sure got *me* motivated. I'm good to go for a couple more days, and I'm sure the boys and everyone else up here tonight feels the same way."

With only two days left to find Wendell's chain, and predictions of a big snowstorm on the way, most of the volunteers decided to stick it out until midnight. Some even decided to work beyond that. After Big John Jacobs found that button, the whole focus of the search had shifted primarily to the upper half down to the mid-section of the giant pine tree.

Every inch of every branch, starting from the top, was being thoroughly searched by more than twenty people, while several others searched the ground around them. Numerous pieces of red material encased in pine sap were found in several locations along the way. The tree was packed full of various sized globs of sap, and each one was yanked, stabbed, prodded, and pulled apart to see if it contained the gold chain. About two in the morning, when the fires were barely a flicker and everyone was just about worn-out, the last volunteers decided to call it quits for the night and head home to get some sleep.

Chapter Eighteen

$\mathcal{A}$t five o'clock the next morning, while Kate filled the kettle with water at the kitchen sink, she stared out the window into the back yard. After she placed the kettle on the burner she opened the kitchen door to the back porch and flipped on the backyard light. The ground was covered in a blanket of snow; not a deep snow, just that thin powdery stuff that swirls on the roads as cars go by. Several minutes later, John snuck up behind her, grabbed her around the waist, and kissed her on the back of the neck.

"Good morning, Babe."

"John, you scared the daylights out of me," she squealed, lightly slapping his arms still wrapped around her.

"Take a look out in the yard, said Kate, disappointedly."

"Oh, great, I was hoping this snow would hold off for a couple more days until we found that chain. Bob and I will just have to take a couple brooms up with us this morning to sweep this stuff out of the way so we can continue the search."

"So what's the weatherman been saying?" Kate inquired.

"He said it would be below freezing today; probably in the low twenties with the wind chill factor. Let's just keep our fingers crossed that it doesn't actually get down that low."

"Wow, Bob, can you believe it's going to be Christmas Eve tomorrow?" John said, as they started brushing off the thin layer of snow from all the branches. "Let's see. It's about eight in the morning, so that gives us forty hours to find that gold chain, get it to Sam so he can turn back into Wendell, then get him back up here to meet Santa Claus before midnight."

"How did we ever let the girls talk us into this one, John?"

"It's not just us, Bob, the boys and our wives have successfully convinced most everyone in town that Wendell is one of Santa's elves. I have never in my life seen so many people so full of the Christmas Spirit. I wouldn't be surprised if half the town showed-up here tonight. It seems that everyone I've talked to lately would love to come up here and help us. Everyone wants to be the one who finds that magical gold chain."

Deep down inside, they both wanted the boys to be the ones to find the chain. After all, they were the ones who started all this, they're the ones who should reap the benefits for being the heroes. To the one who finds the chain, a new legend would be born and forever carved in this town's history.

At about ten thirty, the sun finally found its way through the clouds, the wind died down, and the snow slowly began to melt. By noon, the ground was completely clear again. While John and Bob were standing around the fire pit, warming their hands, they heard someone calling out their names.

"John? Bob? You guys up here?"

"That sounds like Jimmy Smith," Bob said.

When they walked over to the path leading across the plateau, sure enough, there was Jimmy Smith with a crowd of people following close behind.

"Well, I'll be," John chuckled.

Jimmy Smith was accompanied by half the shop owners from Main Street: Hank Parker from the shoe repair shop, Kent James from the camera shop, Larry Grover from the bank, Terri Moss from the dry cleaners, and at least a dozen more. As they got closer, Marylou

Burns from the Main Street Bakery yelled out, "I'm only here to take orders, so don't you two start planning any work details for me!"

"Hi, Marylou," John said, as he gave her a big hug. "Taking orders for what?"

"I've got five of my girls down at the Bakery who have volunteered to stay over tonight to make donuts for everyone who'll be working up here. So, John, my question to you would be, how many should we make?"

"Wow, Marylou, that's going to be a big order. Last night we had over a 150. The night before that there were about 100 or so, and the night before that about 50, so your guess is as good as mine. The word is spreading, Marylou. Kids and adults alike ... we could see close to 200 people up here tonight."

"Okay then, 400 it'll be. That way, if 200 people *do* happen to show up, you'll get two each."

"That's a lot of donuts, Marylou. How on earth are you going to be able to make that many donuts by tonight?"

"Actually, John, the girls and I started making them about seven o'clock this morning. Kate told me earlier that the way things have progressed over the last couple nights that you'd probably have about 200 volunteers tonight."

"So you walked all the way up here just to see if my number was consistent with hers?"

"No," Marylou giggled, as she gave John a hug, "I just needed a break from making all those donuts and decided to come up to see what this place looked like. Every day people come in to the bakery telling me all kinds of stories about what's been happening up here, and I just wanted to see for myself."

"Well, John," Jimmy Smith interrupted, "the rest of us came up here to do some work. Where do you want us to start?"

"Follow me guys," John replied, as he led them past the piles of wood from the cabin, toward the giant pine tree.

Their search began about ten feet from the tip of the tree where John and Bob left off. Within the hour, more and more people arrived, which forced John and Bob to hold off on their own search in order to direct others who were helping for the first time. When Josh, Billy and their moms arrived, they were shocked at the number of people who showed up to help.

"We should have left our car at home and walked up here," Kate joked, as she kissed John on the cheek. "John, you're cheek is as cold as an icicle. Why don't you go stand by the fire and warm up a little before you catch pneumonia."

Before the boys began their own search for the day, they, along with several other kids, began gathering up all the loose brush and branches they could find. There were large piles everywhere that had been accumulating throughout the day. This would be enough to fuel the fire pits for the rest of the night.

By four o'clock in the afternoon, the hours were rapidly counting down. Only thirty-six hours remained until Christmas. The night seemed to fly by once the sun went down. Just after seven, Marylou Burns and her girls from the bakery showed up carrying three to four boxes each, all full of donuts; just as she promised. Following close behind them was a large group of ladies from one of the churches in town, each carrying large Thermoses of coffee and cocoa. Everyone stopped what they were doing and happily greeted them with open arms. They also offered their lawn chairs, while they warmed themselves by the fire pits.

Nearly fifteen minutes went by before anyone started back to work. And even though the donuts, cocoa, and coffee were a welcome surprise, there was still a big job at hand to do; and that was to find Wendell's chain. Unlike the previous night, very few people left at ten o'clock. At twelve o'clock, only a few of the older people left, but by two in the morning, everyone seemed to have finally run out of energy and gathered up their belongings to go home. The vast majority of folks said they would return when the sun came up and would continue straight through to the end of Christmas Eve, if necessary.

As Kate watched them leave, she began feeling guilty about taking advantage of so many families, especially two days before Christmas. *"If we could just find that chain,"* she thought, *"and then all of this will have been worth it."* On the long cold walk back to the car, she thought about Sam. She hadn't stopped by to see him in quite some time, because the only news of any significance she had to share with him was some red material and a button they'd found, and she knew that wouldn't be good enough. After seeing his eyes the last time she, Claire, and the boys left that hospital room, she promised herself that they wouldn't return until someone found something that would make him happy, and only finding the chain could do that.

Chapter Nineteen

Sam opened his eyes and looked around the room to see if any-one was there. As he glanced over at the window, he could see slivers of light poking through the Venetian blinds. "It's daytime," he whispered, "and it's Christmas Eve. Why haven't the boys been by? Even if they haven't found my chain yet, I'd still like to see them. They've been working so hard to help me."

Someone knocked twice and slowly opened the door. "Sam, are you awake?" whispered Nurse Staples. "It's six-thirty, time for your morning checkup."

She wasted no time as she walked directly to the window to let in some daylight.

"It's beautiful outside, Sam. The temperature is in the twenties ... freezing cold, but it sure looks pretty from in here. The weatherman said we might be in for a big snow storm today ..." As soon as she said that, she closed her eyes and bit her lip.

"I'm sorry, Sam. The snow, it ... it'll probably just pass through ... this, this hasn't been a good year for snow. Sometimes we don't get any till almost January."

"That's okay. If it's meant to be, they'll find my chain, Debby, with or without snow."

After she finished her examination, she brought him up to date about what had been happening on the plateau for the last few days and the hundreds of volunteers who had been showing up to help. That was the first time she'd seen him smile.

"Thank you, Debby," Wendell said with a smile, as she walked out the door.

By the time Josh, Billy, and their parents got up to the plateau that morning, there were more than thirty people already hard at work. Young and old were swarming all over the giant pine tree from one end to the other. As the boys walked up to say good morning, they heard a big crack as Big John Jacobs snapped-off one of the branches to make way for a closer search of the lower section of the tree.

"Morning, Big John," Josh said, as he quickly dove to the ground to avoid being hit by the branch that went flying past his head.

"Josh!" Big John yelled, as he ran over to help Josh up. "I'm sorry! I didn't hear you until after I threw that branch. Are you okay?"

"Yeah, I'm OK. You missed me by at least a couple feet."

"Sometimes I get so darn involved in what I'm doing I just block out everything around me. I was so wrapped up trying to find that chain my ears must have stopped working and I didn't hear you coming."

"That's OK, Big John. Say, how long have you guys been at it this morning?"

"About two hours," he replied. "It was dark when we left the house, so we brought up a bunch of lanterns to help us see. Sure is quiet up here in the early morning. This is the last day Josh. We just wanted to get an early start. Don't expect us to leave before midnight though. We have to finish this!"

"Thanks, Big John. You're a good friend."

As quickly as Big John was pulling branches off the tree, Billy and Josh were gathering them up and carrying them off to the fire pits. With more and more branches out of the way, more people were able to get closer to the tree.

About eleven in the morning, Marylou Burns and her girls from the bakery were back, but this time they brought boxes and boxes of Christmas cookies. And not far behind were the ladies from the church again, with another welcome round of coffee and cocoa for everyone.

"Oh boy, coffee," Bob cheered, as he raised his arms in the air. "Thank you, ladies! You must have been reading my mind. I've been craving a hot cup of coffee for the last two hours."

As soon as the words "cookies and cocoa" were heard, all the kids immediately stopped what they were doing and came running.

The day seemed to be whisking by at an alarming rate, but unfortunately, there was still no sign of Wendell's gold chain. Kate continued to pace around the area watching people dig, rake, and claw through the weeds and brush. Occasionally, she would walk over and break off a few of the smaller limbs from the giant pine tree, trying desperately to alleviate some of her frustration.

About four in the afternoon, the mayor strolled up to the plateau with his political entourage carrying dinner for the whole crowd. He had put in a large order for turkey sandwiches with all the fixings at the corner market that morning after he found out what Mr. and Mrs. Wilson had done previously. The mayor didn't like to be outdone by anyone, so this was his way of making his presence known to all the volunteers on the plateau. He also gave a pep talk and wished everyone a Merry Christmas before he grabbed a rake to help out. He loved being the center of attention, even though this was the last day of the search.

When daylight faded into darkness, a faint snow began to fall. Within the hour, the wind started to blow, and the light snow turned into flurries.

"This can't be happening!" Josh yelled. "Why couldn't this hold off for another six hours? If this keeps up, the ground will be completely covered and we'll never find Wendell's chain in time."

Kate assured Josh that the area Big John was working in was shielded from the snow by the overhanging branches from the smaller pine trees. These were the only areas around the tree that hadn't been searched and where the snow couldn't reach.

"There's a good chance that gold chain is within this area, everyone," Big John insisted. "We've got to keep looking."

As the snow continued to fall, people were starting to get frustrated. Within the next hour, more than two inches of snow had fallen, and at least twenty-five people had given up their search and left for home.

Kate and Claire continued searching frantically with the hope that any second someone would yell out that they had found the chain. Shortly after eight, while Kate & Claire were discussing how they were going to break the news to Sam, Billy and Josh started yelling at the top of their lungs. Everybody stopped what he or she was doing and raced over to see what had happened. Before Kate was even able to get around to the other side of the giant pine tree, she could hear people cheering and carrying on. Kate and Claire glanced over at each other as they ran toward the cheering crowd.

"Oh, please tell me they're cheering because someone found the chain!" Kate prayed aloud.

"That has to be it!" Claire yelled. "Why *else* would they be cheering?"

When the crowd parted to let Kate and Claire through, there sat Billy and Josh on the ground holding two large halves of a branch they'd just snapped in two. The branch had snapped in half at the exact spot where, fifty-six years earlier, the chain had fallen onto the branch and became entwined. The branch broke at the weakest part, and the chain was wound in a circular pattern, a couple times on each piece, with only six inches dangling that linked the two halves of the branch together.

"Careful, boys," Bob said, as he motioned to them *not* to move. Keep the branches as close together as you can so the chain doesn't break."

Bob removed the scarf from around Claire's neck and looped it around both pieces of the branch at one end and tied the scarf in a knot. Several other people quickly removed their scarves and threw them to John so he could secure them around the rest of the branch while Bob stripped off all the smaller branches.

"John," Bob said, as he scrambled to pick up the end with the chain, "grab a hold of the other end, and let's get this down to my car. I have some tools in the garage we can use to free this chain from these branches."

Even though the snow continued to accumulate at the rate of at least two inches an hour, the people no longer cared. They gathered up their rakes and other belongings and headed off to the hospital. As they walked across the plateau, they began singing Christmas carols. Kate told John and Bob that she, Claire, and the boys would stop by the house to pick up the box with Wendell's watch, and that they would meet them at the hospital.

By the time Kate, Claire, and the boys arrived at the hospital, however, the parking lot was packed full, and the only place to park was at the emergency entrance. There were people standing everywhere, and several rushed over to greet them as soon as they opened their car doors.

"Just leave your keys in the car and get inside, Kate," Jimmy Smith insisted. "I'll get it parked."

"Thanks, Jimmy," Kate said, as she kissed him on the cheek and rushed into the hospital.

As they raced down the hallway, everyone in town seemed to be lined up on either side of the wall, leaving only a narrow path in the center for one person to pass. When the girls rounded the last corner, they could see Doctor Gaylord standing outside Sam's door.

"We haven't told Sam anything yet, Kate. We've left that up to you and the boys," Mike said, as he pushed the door open. "Go on in."

Except for the light coming in from the hallway, the room was pitch-black. Sam heard the commotion and was already lying with his head propped up on the pillow looking at the door. Claire stood holding the door open while the boys slowly walked toward Sam with Josh carrying the Box. As Josh laid the box on the side table, Sam looked up at Josh and tried to say something, but the words just wouldn't come out.

"We found it Sam. We finally found your gold chain," Josh said, as tears streaked down his face. "Our dads are over at Billy's house getting it freed from one of the big branches we broke off that old pine tree. Apparently when you fell, the chain came off and wrapped itself around one of the branches. Over the years, the tree grew around the chain and hid it inside, kind of swallowing it up. Luckily, Billy and I found it while we were breaking branches to use for firewood."

"I knew you boys would find it. I just knew it," Sam said, as he too began to weep ...

"We got lucky, Sam ... Very, very, lucky," Billy said.

About twenty minutes later, Bob and John came charging into the room. The boys were standing beside the bed as Bob looked at them with a big smile on his face.

"Hi Sam," Bob said, as he reached across the bed and handed him a white folded handkerchief.

The room began filling up with nurses, doctors, and several of the volunteers. They all wanted to be with Sam when he reconnected his chain to his watch. He carefully unfolded the white handkerchief one corner at a time. When he folded back the last corner, the glare from the gold chain gave off a shine that reflected off his face. As tears of joy fell from his cheeks, he slowly raised the chain to his lips and kissed it. Billy walked over, picked up the box from the side table, and stood next to Josh.

"Are you ready to go home, Sam?" Josh asked, as he reached over to open the lid.

"I've been waiting for this moment for fifty-six years. Yes boys, I'm ready."

Josh opened the lid, carefully pulled out the watch, and handed it to Sam. He held the watch in his left hand and the chain in his right for several moments before he actually tried to screw the threaded end of the chain into the diamond tip of the watch. On his first try, he couldn't quite get the chain properly aligned. After the second failed attempt, Billy asked if he needed help. He looked up at him with those helpless eyes and, without a word; Billy grabbed the chain, threaded it into the watch and quickly handed it back to Sam.

The room immediately grew silent as all eyes were focused on Sam. Several seconds passed before anything actually started to happen. Suddenly, Josh and Billy noticed the hands on the watch as they began spinning backwards. With every revolution, they spun faster, and soon, they were turning so fast they just became a blur. That's when it happened. Right before everyone's eyes, Sam's appearance started to change. The side of his face affected by the stroke instantly went back to normal. Then his wrinkles began fading, his ears grew pointy, and his hair and beard grew longer. Then a forest green stocking cap, with a red furry brim and a matching ball at the end, magically appeared on his head.

Sam sat still for a moment and looked around the room. Then in one swift motion, he threw back the covers and leaped out of bed. He was wearing a white long sleeve sweater with a green and red scarf around his neck, bright red knickers with dark green suspenders, and black shiny shoes with green and red striped socks that tucked up under his knickers. As soon as he hit the floor, he began dancing around and singing in a strange elfin dialect that no one could understand.

Josh and Billy walked over to where Sam was dancing and stood right in front of him. Suddenly, he stopped dancing and looked up into their eyes.

"Hi, Wendell," Josh said, as though he were introducing himself to him for the very first time. "I'm Josh; it's nice to finally meet you."

Wendell wrapped his arms around both boys and gave them a big hug. "Hi, Josh and Billy, I'm Wendell, and it's nice to finally meet you, too."

Everyone in the room started to clap and cheer. Soon Wendell was walking around, shaking everyone's hand and giving hugs. The folks in the hallway were just starting to get the news that Sam had turned into Wendell the elf, and suddenly cheers could be heard echoing throughout the building.

"Quiet, everyone," Kate shouted. "Wendell, what time did you say you were going to meet Santa, and where will he find you?"

"One minute before midnight. Once Santa sees me standing in the clearing up at the plateau, he'll come down to get me."

"What clearing, Wendell?" Billy asked. "There's no clearing up by the cabin. That whole area is all over grown with weeds and vines."

"Are you telling me that none of you have ever traveled over to the clearing where the plateau ends?"

Several people looked around at each other and shrugged their shoulders.

"I've never traveled across to that side of the plateau," Jimmy Smith said. "Miss Millie usually got pretty upset with me, even before I could set foot on that log bridge."

"Millie was like that," Wendell laughed. "She always did keep a close eye on that bridge. It was like the *forbidden pass* for anybody but her and me. She probably continued guarding it long after I was gone."

Just then, Big John Jacobs pushed his way through the crowded hallway and into the room.

"Sorry to barge in on you, folks, but I thought you might want to know that the snow is coming down pretty hard out there, and the roads are getting bad. The snow isn't going to be letting up, and the weatherman said that big storm is closing in."

"We have to get going, Wendell," Josh insisted. "We only have an hour and a half to get you back up to that plateau, and you're *not* going to miss this!"

While most of the townspeople began to file out of the hospital and rush off to their cars, Wendell stayed behind with the boys.

"Josh and Billy, I'd ... I'd like to ask you two a favor, if I could."

"Sure, Wendell, anything," Josh said, "What's on your mind?"

"Well, my carvings and all my other belongings ... I can't take them with me. Would you keep them for me?"

"Of course we will, Wendell. We'll make sure that they'll always be protected, we promise."

When they finally got outside, the cars in the parking lot across the street looked like silhouettes buried beneath thick blankets of snow with small drifts that partially covered the tires. Shadows of lit buildings in the distance were mere specks on the thick-blowing wall of snow.

As the boys and Wendell stepped out from under the overhang of the hospital, they sank halfway up to their knees in the snow. But, while they were making their way through the parking lot to Kate's car, Big John Jacobs came driving up with his Case tractor plowing a path for them. Right in back of him was a line of cars with Bob and John leading the way.

"Hop on in you guys," yelled Bob from the open window, "Big John's going to lead the way for us."

The boys, Kate, Claire and Wendell quickly piled into the car.

As Big John plowed a wide path across town leading toward the plateau, a long line of cars followed close behind. It was like a winter parade in progress; with horns blaring, Christmas cheers being yelled out of car windows, and people coming out of their houses to see what all the commotion was about. Crowds stood by the side of the road and waved as the caravan drove by. Some knew what was going on, while others just assumed this was a bunch of the townspeople driving around in the snow storm on Christmas Eve having a good time.

When the caravan reached the top of Millie's dirt road, Bob waited until Big John plowed to the bottom of the hill before he decided to release the brakes. The road was icy under the snow and he didn't want to cause a pileup at the bottom of the hill. All the other cars that followed took caution as well. Big John cleared a path to within a few feet of the log bridge and then shut his tractor down. Bob parked just beyond Millie's house and everyone piled out of the car.

Wendell stepped out first and stared across the snow-covered yard at Millie's front porch. Through the left porch window he could see the drapes pulled to one side and the silhouette of a person peeking out. Kate walked over and put her hand on his shoulder. She knew he wanted to see Millie one last time.

"Hurry up, Wendell. There's only forty minutes left before midnight."

Wendell took off running without saying a word. He seemed to glide over the deep snow as he crossed the yard and was half way up the stairs before Kate could blink an eye.

"Wow!" Billy yelled, as he shimmied across the back seat to get out. "Did you see that, Mom? He ran clear across the top of the snow without sinking in!"

While cars converged on the snow-covered dirt road and the sounds of hundreds of car doors slamming filling the air, Millie slowly opened the front door. Wendell waited in anticipation as she stepped closer to the screen door and into the light.

"Wendell ... Wendell ... is that really you? Is that my Wendell? I thought I'd never see you again. You haven't changed a bit! You look just like you did when I first met you. But, how could this be? I must be dreaming."

"My chain, Millie ... the boy's, they found my gold chain."

Wendell opened the screen door, and Millie stepped out. And as the wind blew and the snow swirled around the front porch, Millie and Wendell embraced.

"Where have you been all these years, Wendell? I've missed you so much. I thought something terrible had happened to you."

"I've been living at the Woodhaven Nursing Home. I was getting too old, Millie, and I couldn't take care of myself any longer. I knew if I told you where I was going, you would have wanted me to stay here so that you could take care of me, and I didn't want to burden you."

"But, Wendell, I wanted us to grow old together. We could have taken care of each other, but now you're back to the young Wendell I met all those years ago, and I'm just an old lady."

"Millie, do you remember when we were younger? I told you that when I found my gold chain, I would take you back home with me?"

"Yes, Wendell, I remember, but I'm too old. I can't go with you now."

"Millie," he said, reaching for her hands, "if you were young again, would you go with me?"

"You know I would, Wendell. There's nothing in this world that I would like more, if only it were possible."

Wendell reached into his pocket, pulled out his watch, and placed it into her right hand. Then he looked into her eyes, smiled, and kissed her. Suddenly, Millie took a deep breath. As she looked down at her hands, she could see her skin beginning to tighten up, and the ache in her back and legs had disappeared. Then, she slowly lifted her left hand and touched her face.

"Wendell, my face … it's so smooth. I'm young again, and I can stand straight up without using my cane. I feel wonderful. How did you do this? How did you make me young again, Wendell?"

"It wasn't me, Millie. It was my magical watch and chain. Millie … there's something about me that I've never told you before, I'm …"

"Wendell, I know what you are. I might be a little slow at times, but I've always known you were an elf. I never understood why you didn't tell me before, but I knew you must have had your reasons, so I just kept quiet about it."

"Then, you'll come with me, Millie? You'll come to the North Pole and be with me forever?"

"Of course I will, Wendell," said Millie, as she threw her arms around him. "But what about all my cats, who will take care of them? I can't just leave them here. They'll starve."

"Wendell!" Josh yelled. "We have to go *now!*"

"Kate," Wendell pointed, as he turned around and looked up to where she was standing next to Josh and Billy. "Kate and Claire will find homes for them, Millie. I'm sure there are plenty of people in this town who would love to have one of your cats."

Wendell reached into his pocket and looked at his watch.

"Let's go, Millie. We've only got thirty five minutes to get to the point."

Millie ran back into the house, slipped on her boots, grabbed her coat and gloves and said a quick goodbye to all of her cats. Then she and Wendell quickly ran through the yard to get to the plowed road. The snow was falling so fast that they had a hard time seeing more than a few feet in any direction. Hundreds of the townspeople were walking up the road toward the plateau behind Wendell and Millie as they reached the spot where Josh and their families waited. Millie recognized everyone, but thought she should reintroduce herself to everyone since she didn't think they'd recognize the new, younger version of her.

"I haven't been up to the plateau since before you left, Wendell," she said.

As they started across the log bridge, the owl up in the tree let off a screeching yell and came flying down toward Wendell.

"Billy! It's that owl again," Josh yelled as he started jumping up and over the snow trying to get away.

"Snowflake," Wendell shouted, as the owl swooped down and landed on his arm. "I thought you would have flown away years ago. Say, everyone, this is my good friend, Snowflake."

Wendell quickly pulled out his watch, wrapped the gold chain loosely around one of Snowflake's talons and transformed him back into a youthful owl.

"They're going to love him up at the North Pole," Wendell chuckled, as he kissed Snowflake on the beak.

The trek up the old log trail to the plateau was easy, because the trees blocked out most of the snow. When they reached the top, the snow stood more than one and a half feet deep across the plateau. As Josh and Billy led the way, they tried to pack down as much snow as they could to make travel easier for everyone behind them. They had difficulty seeing where they were going, but since they'd traveled up there so much lately, they could almost close their eyes and walk straight towards the collapsed cabin. Once they passed the cabin and arrived at the giant pine tree, Wendell and Millie took over the lead to guide them to the point where the plateau ended.

The snow continued to fall at a rate of three inches per hour, and with the wind blowing, visibility was almost at zero. About ten minutes after they'd passed the giant pine tree, they came upon a grove of large pine trees with branches that hung down to the ground. Wendell guided the group toward a small opening that led through the trees. Everyone looked up at the massive pines as their branches dipped low from the weight of the snow.

When they finally passed through, the wind stopped blowing, but the snow continued to fall. The area was wide open and completely surrounded by the same large pine trees as the ones they had just walked through. All the trees looked identical and seemed to have grown to the same height.

"Millie and I planted all these trees around 1898. We planted them in this circular pattern to mirror the curvature of the edge of the plateau. This was our secret place. We would come here often to watch the sunset. Then, late at night, we'd sit and gaze up at the moon and stars. Just up ahead is the end of the plateau ... the point, as Millie and I call it. From the point, you can see the stars and moon as they reflect and sparkle off the pond down below."

With only ten minutes left until midnight, hundreds of people were still plowing their way through the path and into the clearing to witness the arrival of Santa Claus. Wendell walked around and began thanking everyone for finding his gold chain. About three minutes to midnight, Wendell grabbed Kate and Claire by the hands and said his last goodbyes.

"Billy and Josh," Wendell announced, "I'd like to personally thank you for finding my journals. If it weren't for the two of you, and your quest for adventure, I'd still be lying in that hospital bed. I'll never forget you for what you've done for me. Thank you."

Suddenly, someone shouted out that there was a bright light coming down from the sky. Wendell turned around, grabbed Millie by the hand, and walked away from the crowd toward the middle of the clearing.

"Are you ready for this, Millie?" Wendell asked, as he turned and waved to everyone.

"Yes," answered Millie, as she stared up at the fast approaching light.

The light in the sky grew bigger and bigger. Then suddenly, everything slowed down. Everyone and everything in sight seemed to stop moving; the snow flakes stood still in mid air; and there was only silence. The light continued to soar down from the sky and stopped just a few feet in front of Wendell and Millie. As the light dimmed, the outline of a sleigh, Santa, and his team of reindeer suddenly appeared. The image was incredible; every little detail could be seen. It was like a fairy tale come true.

While Wendell, Millie, and Snowflake boarded the sleigh, Santa looked toward the crowd and gave a wink. Then with a wave and a Ho, Ho, Ho, they were off. As the light vanished into the night sky, snow started to fall again, and the sound of people talking could once again be heard. As everyone wept, cheered, hugged, and congratulated each other, Big John Jacobs, with his deep baritone voice, began singing. The song was Jingle Bells, the perfect song for the perfect moment. Suddenly, everyone joined in. Christmas Day had arrived, and all was well.

978-0-595-45090-9
0-595-45090-3

Made in the USA
San Bernardino, CA
07 December 2016